The Couple

THOMAS HÜRLIMANN

✝✝

The
Couple

✝✝

TRANSLATED BY EDNA McCOWN

Fromm International Publishing Corporation
NEW YORK

Grateful acknowledgment is made to Pro Helvetia,
the Swiss Council for the Arts, for its
support of this work.

Translation Copyright © 1991
Fromm International Publishing Corporation, New York

Originally published in 1989 as *Das Gartenhaus*
Copyright © 1989, Ammann Verlag AG, Zürich, Switzerland

Designed by Jacques Chazaud

Printed in the United States of America

First U.S. Edition

Printed on acid-free paper

Typeset by PennSet, Inc., Bloomsburg, PA
Cover printed by Keith Press, Inc., Knoxville, TN
Printed and bound by R.R. Donnelley & Sons Co.,
Harrisonburg, VA

Library of Congress Cataloging-in-Publication Data
Hürlimann, Thomas, 1950–
[Gartenhaus. English]
The couple / Thomas Hürlimann ; translated by Edna
McCown. — 1st U.S. ed.
p.   cm.
Translation of: Das Gartenhaus.
ISBN 0-88064-125-8 : $16.95
I. Title.
PT2668.U667G3713   1991
833'.914—dc20   90-22488

ISBN 0-88064-125-8

The Couple

I

His son died young, even before he reached officers training school. A rosebush, the Colonel said, would be a lovely and fitting reminder of a life that had ended too soon. But Lucienne, his wife, wanted nothing to do with a rosebush—a gravestone belonged there, of granite. He yelled, she sobbed. After long days of silent mourning they could speak again, they fell into each other's arms, they felt guilty, they were old and had survived their son, their only son. The Colonel insisted on the rosebush, she on the stone. He spoke with a gardener, and that very same day Lucienne went up into the mountains, driven there by Ossi Rick, a young sculptor. When she returned home late that night her black stockings were spattered with clay, and the Colonel could have sworn that he heard his grief-stricken wife singing in the shower. He knew that he had lost the battle. It was winter, the ground was frozen solid down to the coffin—it would be spring before he could plant his rosebush. So he sank back down into mourning, a twilight state that lasted for days. Lucienne stayed at Rick's studio. She said she wanted to see the gravestone materialize from the rough rock. Then one icy afternoon it was finished. The Colonel, ordered to the gravesite by his wife, couldn't believe his eyes. A crane was standing behind the cemetery wall, there was yelling, and suddenly the sun went in and something that looked like an elevator car suspended in mid-air rose up over the wall making a humming sound, it swung up higher and higher and then, directed by loud shouting, it descended from the sky, there was a grinding sound, a splintering of wood—the gravestone had landed on its concrete pedestal. Three men released the steel cables, tossed them into the air, and seconds later they were swinging away over the cemetery wall.

Stones of this size were not actually allowed, his wife said to him, but she had been able to get the cemetery officials to make an exception, out of respect for him and his regiment.

He looked up at the crane operator, he didn't understand a word.

"After we die," she continued with a smile, "all of our names will be engraved there, mine and yours as well. But you, mon cher, pose a particular problem—you require more space than our son or myself."

The Colonel was startled.

"Your rank," she said, "your regiment!"

"What is left of it?" he asked.

"Nothing," she said, "but after your name and the dates of your birth and death, we must also carve your rank and regiment."

A power saw whined in the woods nearby. He stared at his wife. Each deceased person gets only one line, she had added, and no more. He jammed his fists into the pockets of his leather officer's coat and, looking up, saw the crane operator hanging by his hands from his cabin. But it was odd—it wasn't the daredevil gymnast in the sky but he himself, standing with both feet planted firmly in the earth of the grave, who suddenly felt dizzy. The man, the crane, and the cabin circled the bleached bubble that was the sun, faster, ever faster, whirling and swirling and whirring, a weeping willow swept by, then Lucienne, and then there was a loud crash. The Colonel gasped. His dizziness subsided. He was still on his feet, thank God. An invisible breaker had dashed him onto the granite rock, onto the gravestone of his son. He ran his fingers over the inscription like a blind man. "Good work," he said hoarsely, "damned good work."

"Thank you," Lucienne said, and tromped over to the sculptor in her Persian lamb coat, unbuttoned despite the cold. He was standing with the workers, a pipe in his mouth. At this, the Colonel left the cemetery and without even noticing it went out into another country, into a new life.

How does disaster begin?

By concealing its beginnings. It creeps up on us, adapts itself to us, and the moment we perceive its twisted features, they laugh at us. It's too late, disaster whispers.

Lucienne left the house every afternoon, once the gravestone had been set in place. She was going to see her son, she said, and the Colonel took her at her word. He sat in his chair for hours looking out at the lake, freight trains clicked past in the distance, the sea gulls wheeled by, and the air grew milder. She returned home only after it got dark, smiling, and would sit down on the sofa and pull off her rubber boots. She wore a gardening apron under her raincoat, and on her head a straw hat or a clear plastic hood, depending on the weather. She wouldn't dress like that if she were visiting an artist, the Colonel thought. But he was nagged at by doubt anyway, by a slight suspicion. She smelled of perfume and wore lipstick, and one evening the Colonel decided to go to the cemetery to inspect the plants at the grave. Lucienne was kneeling before the piece of granite, humming a children's song and setting bulbs into a row of holes she had dug. It looked as if a storm were brewing, the Colonel said, he had brought her an umbrella. She threw him a look over her shoulder, smiling up at him. He withdrew then, walked around the funeral chapel, and sat down on a park bench beneath an old linden tree. The cemetery rose up the hillside in broad plateaus, and was surrounded by a high wall. It had been established, far away from people, during the plague years, but the city had begun to grow at the end of the last century, and its one-family dwellings and apartment houses now were so close to its dead that occcasionally a child's cry leapt the wall bright as a ball. The funeral chapel was almost always in use, his son too had lain there in the coolness scented with flowers and incense, a coolness created by generators that rumbled day and night. He felt a hand on his shoulder. She was finished with her work, Lucienne said. They sat next to each other on the bench for a while. Then the first heavy drops fell, the Colonel opened the umbrella, offered her his arm, and gallantly allowed his wife to precede him out of the east gate. "Age after beauty," he said.

The next day, without discussing it, they left the house together, and soon they were walking to the grave as if it were an old beloved custom. They were the parents of a dead son. They had survived their heir, the bearer of the family name and inheritance, the one who was to have carried the family into the future. It was contrary to nature. Partly out of grief and partly as penance, they paid silent tribute to that with their daily visit to the cemetery.

And it became summer and the summer became hot, and every day at three, the hour on Good Friday that Christ had died, they took tea in the study. Then the Colonel would issue their marching orders and they would set off for the grave arm-in-arm, and from time to time, if Lucienne felt it necessary, the Colonel would hang over his shoulder his golf bag, which held a child's rake and pick in place of his clubs. He helped his wife with the gardening now and then. He would go to the fountain and fill the watering can with water. Or kneel at her side in the flowers and pull weeds. But mostly he would sit on his bench, with the golf bag or umbrella between his knees, and think about this or that, half-awake and half-asleep. Was he dreaming? The Colonel gave a start. It was an evening in late August. No, he hadn't been dreaming, he had fallen asleep. He then hurried to the grave, looked for her at the fountain. "Lucienne," he called, "Lucienne, where are you?"

She had gone home. He stood there helplessly, perhaps for only a second, perhaps for several long and anxious minutes, and something thin and bony and trembling cautiously crept out from behind the gravestone and looked at him with its big eyes.

How does disaster begin?

The Colonel sat alone evenings at the long table at which the family had once dined. Now and then he heard a soft whimpering upstairs—

his wife's grief did not subside with darkness, it increased. He thought of his son and of military maneuvers long past. He drank a bottle of whiskey, smoked a pack of cigarettes, he was hungry and had no appetite. So almost without noticing, he took up an old soldier's habit. Each morning he stuck some rations in his pocket and helped himself to them whenever his stomach dictated.

The animal snatched at it and disappeared behind the granite rock.

One night Lucienne came to his room. The Colonel laughed, and turned off the light so that she would not see his face. It was the first time they had slept together since their son's death, he breathing heavily, she crying.

And the animal became tame, patient, and if he missed a feeding it didn't seem to matter to her. Everything went smoothly those first few weeks. The Colonel would take pruning shears from his pocket and step behind the gravestone. He wanted to get rid of the snails, he had said, but not with poison, he hated poison, he would snip the snails in two.

"You and your aversion to snails," Lucienne said.

She asked him not to kill them in her presence, then she would sit on the bench under the linden tree, or at the edge of the fountain, and if a widow came along to fill a vase, would offer to help her, smiling. One thing would lead to another, the widow was mourning her husband, Lucienne her son, and the Colonel, safely out of everyone's sight behind the pompous monument, could go about depositing food for his animal in peace. Sometimes he heaped dirt over it, and finally he buried the daily ration one or two centimeters below the surface, in the earth around the grave. The next day, when he looked, there was nothing there, and in the course of two months the trembling, miserable creature had turned into a well-nourished cat.

He took meat and leftovers from the refrigerator and smuggled them to the grave in his jacket pocket. Once a trooper, always a trooper. He was and remained front-oriented, he focused his entire concentration on the front, but he could not control those forces at work behind his back, as soon was to be seen. He was cautious at the grave, he considered his every move, this was the front, nothing could surprise him here. When he saw the cat approaching, he gave their marching orders.

"Shall we go?"

"Let's go."

But the Colonel misjudged his wife's parsimonious eye. He would nonchalantly take a slice

of the Sunday roast, stuff a sausage into his
pocket, or half a pound of liver, a little ham, and
one afternoon he took half the ground beef she
had bought that morning.

"Are you eating raw meat?" Lucienne asked.
The Colonel denied it.

"Then the butcher is gypping us," she said.
He nodded. He had never trusted the man,
he said, and they decided to buy their meat and
sausage at the supermarket from then on—he had
jumped from the frying pan, as they said in the
army, but the situation was critical, more dangerous than before. For he needed supplies, and
how was he to get the daily ration he required
behind her back?

I'm an old man, the Colonel thought. I have
a right to certain eccentricities. He went into the
city every morning and drank a glass of red wine
or a whiskey at the City Bar du Boeuf, and
bought the food he needed on the way home. He
hung his officer's coat in the closet.

"You're getting old," Lucienne said, and she
smiled.

He had been to the supermarket, the Colonel
said, to buy cigarettes. Then he swallowed, and
his swallow sounded like a suppressed knock. It
was a brilliant parry—the package of cat food was
only a bit larger than a pack of Gitanes.

She had thrown the stuff away, she said.

What stuff?

Oh, nothing, nothing, Lucienne cooed, and the Colonel had to promise her that he would consult an eye doctor soon.

"I must have picked up the wrong package," he added.

The days were getting cooler, fog was forming on the lake, and Lucienne asked her husband to give up his morning walks. He obeyed. He was stockpiling meat inside the house.

The Colonel knelt down behind his son's gravestone and pushed the daily ration into the damp clumps of earth. It was cool, it was clear, and still light. Lucienne was working on the other side of the granite block. She apparently was trying to scrub the chiseled letters clean with a soap solution; a hint of verdigris had darkened the name. Decay came so quickly, the Colonel thought. The thing had swung down from the sky six months ago, and if you believed the grave diggers, it took a corpse nine months for everything decomposable to decompose; that period had now passed.

"Are you making progress, dear?"

She was scrubbing to no avail, he knew that. Gradual decay was stronger than Lucienne and her solution.

She had gotten as far as the nine, Lucienne called. That would be the nine of the century. What remains of us when we die—a name, a number, and our bones under the earth. He had grown up in the mountains. There they had ground the old bones they dug up from graves into powder; they spiced their Sunday coffee with it, and if someone was dying they took it as their last medicine. He listened to the steady scrubbing sound of her brush, he heard her breathing— between them stood the gravestone that concealed them from each other. Would they cease being strangers to each other there, at its base? Lucienne was the daughter of a textile manufacturer, an arrogant egoist, and he himself had come down from the mountains a lifetime, a long time, ago. Homesick? He had objected to the stone's size, but now, as so often in his life, the defeat he had suffered was compensated for in a marvelous way. This rock that she had put there against his orders offered him the protection he needed. Here, between the back of the monument and the cemetery wall, he could carry out his duty undisturbed. He pressed down harder with the heel of his hand on a piece of meat buried in the earth, then he got up, bent over the stone as if over a parapet, and looked down at his wife, kneeling and scrubbing. All Souls' Day was in three weeks, she had said, and by All Souls' she wanted to have the stone clean.

"What are you thinking about?"

Nothing, the Colonel said, he wasn't thinking about anything. Somewhere in the cemetery a candle was lit, someone snapped off a dead stalk, someone stood at the fountain and filled a vase with water. He took his gloves from the neighboring gravestone and put them on. Then he nodded in greeting to the cemetery's gardeners, squatting in front of the chapel like beggars banished outside the gate. They were smoking cigarettes, one of them was eating an apple. A couple of them nodded back, and suddenly the crane operator materialized before his eyes, the one who had lifted the stone up over the cemetery wall. The conquering hero type, the Colonel thought, a Communist, of course, rather slant-eyed, chin jutting forward, a red star on his fur cap. When had that been? Officers school in Walenstadt during the Cold War, it was sizzling in the conference room, but they weren't allowed to unbutton their uniforms—gentlemen, here you see the enemy, this is what he looks like, next slide, and there was a click and the projector threw a tank driver up on the wall, then a pilot, a gunner, an infantryman, an endless gallery, an entire regiment, Mongols, Kirghiz, Georgians, all wearing fur caps with red stars. Lights, Attention! Comrade Kessler, who remained seated—he had slept through all of the Ivans—was put in the stockade for twenty-four hours, Zollikofer showed no mercy. Zollikofer, the Colonel said, he was thinking about Zollikofer.

He knocked on the gravestone as if on wood. He considered himself fortunate, after all these years, to be able to remember how many hours Kessler had spent in the stockade. The few visitors to the cemetery had disappeared, the gardeners were pushing their wheelbarrows full of leaves out through the west gate, and in the twilight haze the cemetery became a land without borders, a gray planet. It looks, the Colonel thought, as if the atom bomb had already been dropped here, and for a moment he surrendered himself to the thought that in the kingdom of the dead even the future was the past. But then it occurred to him, making him break into a sweat, that he himself was subject to time and catastrophe, the minutes burning like a lit fuse, faster and faster. His cat arrived on the dot. She appeared at the grave of Emilio Hagedorn, heart attack, a shadow creeping around the light-colored marble, seconds later she glided past the holy-water font of comrade Kessler, a prostate affair with a fatal post-operative ending, and half a minute later the red storm lamp on the Zurlauben family grave reflected off a furry coat gliding silently by.

Lucienne was still scrubbing. He stepped from behind the stone and stood on the gravel path.

"Shall we go?"

She continued scrubbing. Here and there a light sputtered in the damp air, red or yellow, a lantern or a candle, and the Colonel turned his head cautiously. Had she already passed the Zurlaubens?

Then he saw her, she was approaching, alert phase one. Three minutes more and she had reached, via Hagedorn and Zurlauben, the so-called jungle, the fleshy covering of leaves over the Siegenthalers' graves, he of stomach cancer, she of intestinal, where the cat, only three arms'-lengths away, waited between the two urns, crouching on the ground, a pitch-black ball, sniffing the air perhaps, but otherwise motionless, absolutely motionless. Only an experienced watchman would be able to make out two green slits in the jungle darkness—her eyes reflecting the twilight sky.

She was a wild cat, the tip of her tail was flat

like a tiger's, and her little nose was pink. She must have come from the woods nearby, drawn there by the flesh rotting on bones in the coffins. But she seemed to fear the living, she avoided them, crouching there silently, she could wait, and only when the Colonel and his wife left the grave would she dash from the jungle and spring behind the stone, to begin digging. But wasn't it possible that she would lose her shyness one day? The Colonel drew his glove across his forehead, it was wet with perspiration. He felt a chill. There was a rustling in the jungle, she was there, the sky was red and the cat's eyes burned red as sparks, close enough to touch. He knew that at some point she would step forward, purring, and in that instant he would lose his wife. "Our dead son," she said on occasion, "has brought us back together again."

Their son? No, the Colonel thought. It was duty that brought him to the grave. In his old age, he, the former soldier, had become a supply officer for a stray cat.

II

She had no memory of her mother. Her father was proud that the *Laetitia* looked like a warship—that had been her father's marvelous idea—there was nothing superfluous on board, no women, no pictures, no animals. Lucienne wore a little sailor's suit. The meals were served by a manservant, a male secretary sat in the ante-room keeping strict control over house and park. She had been a happy child, she later said. She played in the park, threw balls up in the air, and stuck out her tongue at the underlings who hurried back and forth between the *Laetitia* and her father's factory. If her father was away on a business trip—his secretary would say: "We are overland"—she would beg the servant for the key to the attic and sneak out onto the roof to look at the gables and church towers of the city. When I grow up, she is reported to have said, I want to be a woman like this city. Her father wrote down this childish saying on a piece of paper. She found it under his desk blotter shortly after his death. That's right, her father had written on the back of the paper, All my best, Your Father.

Lucienne spent seven years in a convent school in Italy. The girls wore navy blue pinafores, and on Sunday evenings they were allowed to gather around the radio in the recreation room. Colored points of light glowed on the radio's tuning dial and the green bands looked like the silhouettes of skyscrapers in some distant city. That's what New York would look like, Lucienne thought, if you approached it by sea, standing on the bow with the wind in your hair. The girls lived in halls—halls for sleeping, dining halls, study halls—and the long whitewashed hallways stayed cold even in the summer. To the envy of all of her friends, she quit a year before graduating—Lucienne went to war.

It was cold, she said later, bitterly cold on the platforms, and almost even colder in the waiting rooms where the Red Cross nurses awaited the arrival of trains from far away, stirring keg-sized kettles of tea, buttering bread, snacking on the sugar. Lucienne wrote long letters to her father. She repeatedly asked him for a picture of her mother, but the replies he dictated to his secretary ignored her request. Her father notified her that he had questions of his own, now that he had been cut off from the exporting business, and in these hard times they must be given precedence. He asked her to provide him with a detailed description of the German train personnel, he would enter trade negotiations with the Reich soon, it hadn't yet been approved, it was true, but he was confident, All my best, Your Father. She again urgently requested a picture, or a piece of jewelry, or anything of her mother, but her descriptions of the coats, waistless jackets, gloves, and even the red scarves of the German railway men were as precise as this longing was vague.

One July night she started a conversation with a locomotive engineer as she had handed him a bowl of tea. The old man admitted to wearing a neckerchief of Chinese silk—it was a relic of better days, he said, under the Kaiser he had been the conductor of the Berlin-Hamburg stock-exchange train.

Her father praised her in his next letter. An

excellent description, my child. It was clear that they were now using retirees in order to keep the younger men readied for new assignments and territories. He calculated that Hitler would invade Russia, All my best to you, Your Father.

Her father had purchased tons of wool yarn on the same day that he had received her letter, and switched to the manufacture of headbands, lined caps, and mittens. Some of our wares, Lucienne was later to say, survived the trenches of the great battles—it was entirely possible that one or another of their products was still being worn in the Siberian camps today.

She became ill during the third winter of the war. She was brought home, and for weeks alternated between chills and fever and a pleasant fog of sleep, fever, and dreams. When she came to, she found on her night table the notice of her father's death, signed by her. He had caught his daughter's flu, sitting at her bedside, and perhaps had died the death that had been meant for her. The doctor who saved Lucienne was mobilized shortly thereafter, and took her along as a field nurse. She was happy that her blue-and-white uniform spared her having to dress in mourning—she wore a black button on her chest, nothing further was required. Nor was there a burial; her father, though Catholic, had requested in his will that he be cremated, and in May of 1945, as the barrier bars were raised at the border, his secretary set out on a long journey with a small zinc case. It was said that the customs men had laughed—one of the first to leave the country was taking two pounds of ashes out into a Europe that had been decimated. But that too had been in the will, typical of Papa, and though nothing was ever heard again from the man with the case, it was assumed that he carried out the last will and testament. The master of the *Laetitia* wished to be scattered over the seven seas.

In the army hospital, Lucienne, who now wanted to live, to live at last, and laugh, became intimately familiar with boredom and senseless longing. The beds remained empty. The doctors guzzled schnapps. The nurses sang songs. Ennui. Hypocrisy. Her father was dead, she had inherited his property, and Lucienne often caught herself wishing that the operating tables were filled with bleeding men. She envisioned quivering stumps of arms sticking out from shoulders. She got hold of newspaper articles on the army at Stalingrad—it had been defeated during her illness—and devoured the news from the front as eagerly as she once had her father's letters. She had herself fitted for boots, took riding lessons,

and dreamed of riding into Siberian captivity at
the side of the great Field Marshal General Paulus,
commander of the defeated Sixth Army. Lucienne, hungry for life and death at the same time,
experienced bitter afternoons when nothing at all
happened, and yet time went by. She would have
nothing to do with the army doctors. She read,
she rode, and in the early winter of 1945 a young
lieutenant, also on horseback, crossed her path
in a forest clearing drenched in sunlight. The
young man could not possibly know anything of
her assets—her father's factory had been sold in
the meantime—and his sorrel's name was Carlos.
That indicated a knowledge of Schiller, and hence
a good education, and from her father Lucienne
had learned: Our hastiest decisions are our best,
All my best, Your Father.

The lieutenant's column trudged by.

"I'm a nurse, in anesthesiology," Lucienne
said. "May I anesthetize you, Lieutenant?"

Fifteen minutes later he was standing at attention, asking the nurse, who was in the process
of hooking up her stockings, to be the mother
of his future sons.

She loved the evenings spent at the grave, she
was happy here. When she spoke, her words be-

came a prayer, and the work she did there seemed
holy. His life had been short. He had not lived
long enough to appear before his father in uniform, but her scrubbing and scraping at the num-
bers on his grave was taking half an eternity.
Wasn't that nice, wonderfully, wonderfully nice?

He had disappeared behind the gravestone
again. If only she knew how to help him. He
never mentioned their son, had shed no tears at
his deathbed, none at the funeral, but now,
months after their son had died, he got more
eccentric every day. He had just that moment
performed a dance, a dance at the grave. And it
was by no means the first time that he had suddenly clapped his hands and simultaneously
barked out a kind of cough—not to mention the
snails! He was constantly hunkered down behind
the gravestone hunting for snails, supposedly,
groaning now and then, sighing softly. His boots
would creak and his leather coat would crackle,
he apparently had difficulty when he was kneeling
down, moving about in the small space between
the wall and the stone. And would move about
back there anyway and, as he said, whack the
snails in two with his garden shears, but no poison, he said, no snail poison. It could no longer
be denied: his son's death had changed him. It
was true that he accompanied her to the cemetery
every day, faithful as a dog, and that he had given

23

up his morning visits to the pub. But she felt him withdrawing from her more and more—he crept into his own thoughts like a wounded animal into its lair. He scarcely even looked at the *New Zurich News* anymore; up until then he had not only read it, but studied it. What is news anyway, he remarked, there's news every day, and not even the *Swiss Army News*, which in 1965 had praised him as a leader and a soldier, could lure him out of his solitary world. The papers lay under his bed, unread.

"Shall we go?"

"Let's go," and Lucienne would hurry to pack her things into his golf bag. There was the horn— Zizi, their eldest daughter, who drove them home from the cemetery every evening, had pulled up.

He stepped from behind the gravestone like an angel guarding the Holy Sepulcher, she quickly wiped a tear from her eye and took his arm. Despite his age, he was still a stately man. Eccentric, she thought, but that was part of a man's character. Her father, too, had become eccentric as the years went by, he kept his office dark even during the day, and only his globe, a huge ball lit from within, bathed his bald head in blue-green light, like that of an aquarium.

Now they rounded the funeral chapel, and the Colonel turned his head to take one last look at the grave. This too had become a habit, a fancy, a whim, Lucienne would put money on his stopping briefly each time at the corner, to glance back over his shoulder.

Their daughter's Toyota was standing at the east gate—they walked, blinded, toward its headlights.

It was then customary to greet and thank and kiss their chauffeur, and Lucienne performed this with great theatricality. For dear Zizi, their eldest, was at ease, polished and charming, only in social settings; with the family and in her marriage she was a vulnerable creature who was appallingly, seismically sensitive to insult. She collected misfortunes, doubts, sorrow, and mental anguish. She had been pregnant as her brother lay dying. Had Zizi had an abortion? No one knew, not even she, Zizi's mother and best friend. But that was typical of the poor thing! At the time of the alleged abortion the attention of the entire family had been centered on the son, and the subject of Zizi's childlessness had been bitterly taboo ever since. A very thin-skinned person, it occurred to Lucienne now and then. Yes, despite her domineering behavior, despite her howling arias of distress, which betrayed her toughness and strength—that for sure, that above all!—sweet Zizi was one big gaping wound, her muscles twitched visibly, her heart pounded, her lungs gasped for air. Lucienne disengaged herself from her husband's arm and glided toward her thin-skinned daughter. "How nice, you're here!"

"Hello."

"Have you been waiting long?"

She flicked a speck of dust from her daughter's sleeve, clapped her hands, and said, "But no, how good you look today, wonderfully, wonderfully pretty!"

The Colonel had crawled into the back seat, Zizi slammed the car doors shut.

The cemetery came alive in the days before All Souls'. The graves were covered with bunches of fir branches, an angel was cleaned here, a block of marble there, the withered holy-water sprinklers were replaced, and the gardeners spent hours raking the gravel paths. They had shaken the leaves from the trees and collected them, and if one single leaf fell somewhere, a gardener came running to jab it with a pike.

Lucienne had finished her work early. But the Colonel was still waging his daily battle against the snails, there must be hundreds of them, a mass of rust red, slimy, boneless bodies that he snipped in two evening after evening and buried in the earth behind the tombstone. Lucienne didn't say a word. She was glad, almost happy, for several days now he had overcome his lethargy. Scarcely had she brought him the paper before he tore it open, in the evening he sat in front of the radio, and two or three times she had heard him telephoning behind closed doors with a weather station to ask, in his growling commander's voice, when winter would set in. And he was always looking up at the sky distrustfully, almost fearfully—she gave a shudder, it all became clear to her. The first snow had fallen over city and country the night their son had died. What was it he had said then? "It's the cold hand of death, Lucienne. It struck tonight."

And as always, they drank their tea at three in the afternoon and went to the cemetery, and when it began to get dark, heard the sound of their daughter's horn tooting for them. Then they returned to the city in silence, and it was only seldom that they could see the boats anchored in the bight. If they emerged at all from the fog they lay there motionless, like a herd of dead whales. All Souls' was four days away. He was sitting in the back seat, and Zizi was racing along the shore road when he coughed slightly, and Lucienne took this as a sign to inform the Colonel of a decision she had made days before, and had spoken to her daughter about. It was fall, and her husband was no longer of the youngest.

"After All Souls' Day," she said, "we'll cut back on our visits to the grave."

Zizi braked sharply, turned left, and drove into the park of the *Laetitia*—crusted, ancient trunks, and underbrush of dry roots, a carpet of black and moldy leaves. Since the death of their son, the garden had reverted to an enchanted wilderness, Lucienne had let it happen, for much as she would have liked, she didn't have the strength to tend the grave and the park at the same time. The house, with all its towers and contours, stood black against the night. The only light was a reddish glow coming through the trees from the other side of the bight, toward the city. One of the windows of the house reflected like a blind mirror, and in the middle of the wild growth a round tin cupola provided a bit of brightness. It was the summerhouse, the decaying reminder of the happiest days of their lives.

They got out. The lake air smelled like damp diapers, Lucienne observed.

Zizi went into the trees at this, she stepped into the darkness without a word.

Lucienne fumbled in her handbag for the key, and found that she had left it sticking in the lock.

A little while later, Zizi returned. Mercy had won out over justice, and Zizi had decided not to kill herself. Lucienne wished she could express her thanks, and swore to herself never again to use the word diaper in the presence of her child-less daughter. "Would you have dinner with us?"

Thank you, Mama. Unfortunately, she had no time, she said. Next time, perhaps.

Now was the time for prudence, alert phase one, as the Colonel would say. If she went over to her daughter to give her a kiss good-bye, it would offer her the opportunity to interpret the kiss as a signal to leave. If she didn't give her a kiss it would be just as bad, no, even worse: she would be blackmailing her daughter into staying.

She motioned to the open door. The Colonel was sitting in his armchair in the study, his feet wrapped in the plaid blanket, a glass of whiskey in his hand, filled to the brim. She was worried about Papa, Lucienne whispered.

"I must go nevertheless."

"Please, my dear, do whatever you wish."

"Let's go into the kitchen," her daughter said, "we can talk undisturbed there."

"Thank you," Lucienne said.

The next morning the Colonel remained in bed. Lucienne sat at the kitchen table staring at the yellow flecks on the ceiling, then at ten she took him a pot of tea and two pieces of toast. His room was set up like a barracks: bed, table, chair, a sparseness that reminded her of her father— nothing superfluous on board, no women, no pictures, no animals. Nevertheless, for decades her husband had rejected the title he had inherited with the marriage, and only when their son, who was born late, began calling him Capitano did the Colonel give up his objections. It was an honorary title: il Capitano. Lucienne had read in Borges that there is a will that resides in things longer than it does in people, and the *Laetitia*, which considered itself not a house but a ship, was an example of this. Its absurd will, which could be traced back to the seafaring dreams of its previous owner, had transmuted its new master into a captain, though he had been born in the mountains, had commanded a mountain troop, and was totally ill-disposed to nautical fantasies. He sat in his chair, but his night shadow was still lying in the bed. He had sweated it into his sheets, and the damp gray creases looked like wrinkles. She went to the window. In the fall mist the lake appeared as vast as a sea, a waterfowl screeched in the distance, the clock struck downstairs. She put the tray on the night table and closed the door gently behind her.

Lucienne had triumphed over the Colonel— the granite rock, not the rosebush, had been placed on the grave. Roses would fade, but this stone towered like a pinnacle above what was temporal. She had fought for her son, she admitted that openly. Lucienne believed that someone was truly dead only when he had disappeared from the memory of the living, and she was comforted by the thought that in a future time, perhaps the next millennium, a visitor to the cemetery would stop for a moment in front of the moldering grave to read the name of this person who had died prematurely. But that was true of her husband as well, whether he admitted it or not—the stonemason's chisel would see to it that he and his rank and regiment would endure beyond death.

She stopped in the hall. She found her thoughts going in circles. He had suffered a defeat with his rosebush, it was true, and she perceived, she felt, she knew that her husband had not been the same since. He drank. He got drunk, lay back in his chair, and sank into a blissful stupor, a euphoria of dream and reality. He, who had always been an early riser, got up later and later each day, today he hadn't even appeared at breakfast, and with the exception of a sudden burning interest in the weather, his curiosity about the world and its people had faded. It was grief he was suffering from: he had found no way to express his sadness. Or was it even worse? Yes,

Lucienne thought, he didn't even know that he was sad. But the poor man was suffering nevertheless, suffering like an animal, and seemed to have decided to suffer at the stone that she had had put there against his wishes. No, she thought, no, that wasn't it either. For each day the Colonel hurried to the cemetery with almost more resolution than she herself. Was it to experience his defeat each time anew? To whet himself until he bled on this stone, which was a substitute for his grief? She would have expected something like that of her daughter Zizi, Lucienne reflected, but not of her husband. And so it came full circle, the cat was biting its own tail. He saw his own defeat in the stone, and felt strangely comforted in its shadow. He suppressed his grief, but he needed the daily trip to the grave to deal with it. Something wasn't right. She went back upstairs and knocked at his door.

"May I?"

He was still sitting in his chair.

"I know what you are afraid of," Lucienne said.

He shot up, his eyes burned, his forehead turned pale. She saw how he struggled for words that would not come, and then she heard a scream. "Get out, forward, march!" the naked man screamed.

She stumbled backward out the door, too surprised even to close her mouth, dazed—had he struck her with his fist it could not have been worse. Her hand jerked the door shut, just as if she were protecting herself from a predatory beast.

Then she saw the door handle go down, looked at it in horror, and suddenly he was standing in the light that fell from his room into the hall and was grinning—truly, he was grinning. "What is it that I'm supposed to be afraid of?" the man asked.

"The first snow fell the night he died," Lucienne said.

"Why," the Colonel asked, "should an old mountain man like me be afraid of snow?"

He groped his way toward her, put his hand on her back, and pulled her to him.

He had succeeded in becoming a mystery to his wife, but Lucienne doubted that she had the strength, the patience, or the love necessary to solve it. They went together to the grave, they sat together at the table, and in the evenings he lay back in his chair and drank.

On All Souls' Day, all of their daughters and their husbands gathered on the *Laetitia*. *Café complet*, the family called it, and though they had attended

33

a Mass for the dead at an early hour and had visited the grave afterward, they were in a cheerful mood later that morning. Lucienne's sons-in-law honored her with a compliment. Your grave, they said, is a work of art. She was pleased at this. She drank a glass of champagne, and only toward evening did she begin to suspect that the strange floral arrangement at the Siegenthalers' grave—her daughters had made fun of it, but no, how tasteless—could have been orchestrated by the Colonel. Yes, it was obvious: when they mentioned the wild bouquets he had flinched as if caught in the act, the topic was disagreeable to him, he wanted to change it. "Not a word more about the Siegenthalers!" he had called out laughing, but his eyes were ice-cold, full of fear, full of distrust. It frightened Lucienne. Had her own husband become such a stranger to her that she totally misinterpreted an unintentional scowl? Was she seeing connections where there were none? In the end, she thought, I'll be the one who's crazy, and alone there in the study she let out a high, ringing laugh. No, for the life of her, it was too much to suspect of him! It was beyond her power of imagination—the Colonel sneaking around the cemetery in the night and fog, to bury the Siegenthalers' urns beneath a sea of gaudy flowers.

One week after All Souls', Lucienne gathered her courage and said: "I don't want to be responsible for your death."

"Why would you be?"

"You consider it your duty to accompany me every day."

"What does that have to do with my death?"

"Nothing," she said.

He merely shrugged his shoulders, he apparently didn't understand a word. Then she put down her cup and launched into an explanation that she herself realized was convoluted, in which she explained that the cold and damp fall air could be dangerous to his health.

"Forward, march," the Colonel said, "destination, cemetery."

"Admit it, at least," Lucienne screamed.

"What, then? What should I admit?"

"That you cannot deal with your grief."

"To the contrary," he replied, "oh, to the contrary." Then he hung his golf bag over his shoulder and offered her his arm.

III

When the Colonel awoke, his wife was standing at the window and Zizi, his eldest, was lying on the sofa. The two women were discussing marital things, apparently; they weren't paying attention to him. He could hear a faint buzzing in the distance and the glasses rattling slightly in the cabinet—the night shift had begun at Meier-Labiche.

He had buttoned himself up in his wool jacket, and as weak, as frail and drained and demoralized as he had felt on climbing out of the

Toyota two hours earlier, now, after the first three drinks, he felt strong—il Capitano in his armchair, too able, too indispensable, too necessary to the development and well-being of his family to be destroyed by anything short of the end of the world. His hand reached for his glass. He took three or four short sips. Thank God the women didn't notice it. They were involved in a little skirmish, bound to each other in love and hate, hissing quietly, whispering, murmuring, and that was good, it was right—to treat his slumber with respect. He accepted the compliment. When il Capitano is sleeping, the troops are to tread lightly. There was a whirring sound from the next room, then a ding-dong, the first strike, the second, and the Colonel sank down again in a wild swirl of images, half-asleep, half-awake, but throbbing with energy, with the intense vitality of life.

The freight trains rattled and strained at their couplings, horses whinnied and snorted, the locomotive released wisps of smoke, there was the sound of a shrill signal, and though the Colonel knew that Gerber, his orderly, had gone to his eternal bunker years ago, the alleged deceased was busily working his way toward him, forcing the agitated horses apart with punches and flat-handed slaps. Now he saluted and reported with a yell that there had been a delay in loading the horses onto the train.

Two cars ahead, a horse had balked on the loading platform, but the man holding its halter knew what he was doing, and led the devil safely into the car. Its hooves drummed dully, muffled by the straw scattered on the floor. The wind and rain lashed down, the signal lanterns pitched, the Colonel knew that his train had to depart. He was in the car in three leaps, inspecting the provisions, and the men standing with the horses greeted him thankfully. He was one of them, a mountain boy, he knew animals, saw that there were enough oats and straw. He stepped onto the ramp and looked out into the night. It smelled of coal, and apples for the horses, it smelled of war, the situation was serious. Medical orderlies hurried along the train, weighed down by huge crates of bandages, they stumbled in the gravel, a siren sounded in the distance, an air-raid warning, but one horse was still lying on the steep ramp, whinnying, biting, snapping, time was short.

We aren't leaving without this horse! the Colonel screamed.

Yes sir, Gerber affirmed, officers' quarters are at the rear of the train!

Let them make themselves comfortable—I'll ride with the troops.

Yes sir, Colonel sir.

And the horse suddenly found its legs, as if lifted up by magic. At first he thought he heard its hooves on the planks, but that must have been a mistake, an illusion, for the horse, writhing on its back, rose straight up in the air as if it had sprouted wings. And at that same moment, the walls of the cattle cars exploded, the roofs opened, and the Colonel found himself flung up in the fiery eruption along with the dark bodies of the horses. Far beneath him the iron skeleton of the train buckled, the siren ceased, it grew quiet, cool, and not one of the men from the train had abandoned his horse, he could see that. They held fast to the halters, attached to their animals like astronauts to their space capsule.

" 'Bye," said Zizi.

Now his lips were kissing his daughter's cheeks and she was kissing him. Lucienne had raised a window, cool air blew in from the lake, and a little later they heard a dull grinding sound in the park; his daughter was turning the Toyota on the gravel drive, she tapped the horn twice briefly and then drove out to the road, her motor roaring.

"Good night," the Colonel said.

He looked out and up at the sky. Winter was coming, it had been coming for days. When would the first snow fall? That night?

A damned tricky situation. The falling leaves had robbed his cat of its cover, and who knew what would have happened had he not been able to talk the gardeners into blanketing the Siegen-thalers' grave with all the cemetery's leftover flowers. He couldn't bear the sight of urns, he had told them. It doesn't matter how you arrange them, gentlemen, but I cannot look at those vessels any longer. It had cost him a few bottles, no more.

He took in the night air. He had been familiar with winter since childhood, and it was only city dwellers who could maintain that the world disappeared under white snow. To the contrary, snow revealed everything. It made visible the footsteps of humans and the tracks of animals.

The Colonel pushed his chair over to the heater. He filled his glass again, he drank and listened to the fire sputter. Someone has to keep watch, he said to himself, someone must be there.

The first snow fell during the last week in November. The Colonel stopped his supplies. This had been necessary during the war as well, depending on the situation at the front. But the howling and whimpering he had anticipated did not ensue, not on the first, nor the second, nor the third evening, and on the fourth—Lucienne was busy scraping the ice from the holy-water fonts—the Colonel glanced up at the sky. He almost gave away his secret. There! he wanted to shout, there she is, she's still alive. Despite her hunger she had not abandoned her territory, and was crouching quietly on the wall that closed off the cemetery beyond the rows of graves. He happened to have three slices of ham in the right pocket of his coat and a bag of birdseed in his left. He took out the bag, stamped behind the granite rock and, as they left the cemetery together—arm-in-arm as usual—his wife said to him that he was an eccentric but good-hearted man. "Why eccentric?" the Colonel asked.

She giggled, shaking her head. "I watched you," she finally said, "you went behind the grave and scattered seed."

Did she have anything against that?

"No, no," Lucienne said, and began humming a children's song to herself—it's snowing, it's roaring, a chill wind is blowing, all the little birds are cold, and all the little children.

Whether it was that she didn't like the damp snow, or that she didn't want to leave tracks behind—from then on the cat arrived by way of the wall, and once again she arrived after dusk, as punctually and silently as before. She had changed her route from land to air. The snow didn't stick to the slanting bricks, and it was easy for her to dance along the sharp ridge at the top. She paused for a while each time she reached Dossenbach's grave, a long shadow in the twilight, and waited until the Colonel and his wife had departed.

The Colonel, in the meantime, had overcome his fear that Lucienne would one day spot the cat lurking on the wall. The good woman was not getting any younger, her eyes were getting weaker, and a person who is nearing the end of her life seldom looks up at the sky.

At Christmas he received a big package of birdseed—To My Good-hearted Husband, From His Dearest. So that he could feed the birds in the dead of winter as well, Lucienne said, and the Colonel thanked her with a kiss.

New Year's Eve on the *Laetitia*, with all the daughters and their husbands and the entire group of grandchildren, only Zizi sent her regrets, a migraine.

"What's this all about?" Schacht asked.

Lucienne had led him away from the celebration to the daughters' bedroom, and Schacht had followed willingly, of course, he was Zizi's husband.

He snapped open a silver cigarette case and noted with a grin that the two of them, he and Mama, knew of course why Zizi hadn't come.

Her daughters had slept in a long white room. Once a year, in the spring, a cleaning woman polished the floor, aired the beds, and cleaned the cupboards. Otherwise, the room was so empty that it was as if this part of the *Laetitia* had already sunk, it was an abandoned, dead deck. The radiators were turned off, the beds had dust covers, and the wax that the cleaning woman rubbed into the linoleum had saturated the abandoned coolness like a disinfectant. The windows faced south, looking out onto the lake, and the children's white cots stood all in a row along the back wall. Lucienne turned an ear to the hall and then closed the door. She smiled. Her daughters' bedroom reminded her of the hospitals of her youth.

"Shall we stroll up and down a bit?" she asked Schacht, then gave him permission to smoke, and let him know that her reason for wishing to speak with him did not involve Zizi.

"She can't stand the noise," Schacht said, "the noise of children makes her physically ill."

Above each bed hung a charmingly tinted panel, similar to a fever chart, and on each panel the Savior rose up to heaven, and each Savior had a lance piercing his heart, a heart that hung from his robed body like a money sack surrounded by a little shining sun. Below the hem of his robe, rippling in the breeze, a pair of feet hung limply, crossed one over the other, held with a nail, and below them, in india ink, was printed the name of the child who had occupied that bed—her name and the day and year of her first holy communion. Zizi had slept in the first bed by the door. She had been commander in chief of the sleeping quarters—at exactly nine p.m. she ordered everyone to bed, and woe to the sister who was found trying to slip under the wrong blanket!

The Savior above Zizi's bed was pale, almost colorless, and Zizi's name could only barely be made out: sun and time had faded the panel. But the names and dates became more distinct as Lucienne and Schacht moved farther into the room, between windows and beds, the hearts gained in color, and over the last bed, where her youngest daughter had slept, a sun's corona, yellow as butter, surrounded a moist, red, bleeding heart. She was worried about the Colonel, Lucienne said. Very worried.

"I'll always be here for the two of you."

"His grave brought us together again—we've become happy in our old age."

"That's good."

"But dangerous," Lucienne added. "Papa is no longer as young as he used to be, if you know what I mean, and for the last few days the temperature has dropped below freezing."

"May I ask why you're laughing?"

She shook her head. It was so ridiculous, almost insane—there was meat stored in one of the little cupboards, that's right, meat, a plastic bag full of meat. She so would have liked to open one of the little doors and show Schacht the gruesome cache. But was Zizi's husband wise enough to understand what it meant?

The death of their son had pushed her to her limit too, it was true, behind which lay the no-man's-land of insanity, as big as Asia. But compared with the Colonel's meat campaign, the fact that she spent entire nights weeping seemed basically harmless—she had brushed up against her limit and he had leapt over his. She had pulled herself together months ago, it was hard for her in retrospect to understand her feelings. And he? What was he doing? It had been two days before Christmas. He had sneaked into the bedroom, she had followed—he's probably hidden my present here, she thought. She spied on him behind his back. A nice joke! Crazy. What did he need meat for? Why was he storing meat here, in their daughters' bedroom, raw, bloody meat?

"Meat?" Schacht asked.

"Oh, was I talking out loud?"

Zizi has her moods, he continued, and her vegetarianism, her abhorrence of meat—that too was a mood, a fad, you simply had to wait it out, be patient and wait it out. Lucienne let him talk. She knew now that she would not open the cupboard in front of this man. Schacht, like all men, was naive. Sweet, but ignorant of feelings. Zizi's complexity apparently filled him with a certain pride. He, the good Schacht, was man enough to steer his thin-skinned, unstable wife through the straits of banal, everyday life with stoic aplomb. An uncle, not a lover. That was what was destroying Zizi, and Schacht's business was improving quarterly. She can choose the best analyst if she wishes, he liked to say, it's no problem for us financially. Did he see other women? Lucienne looked at him from the side. It's possible, she thought, but not probable.

She had observed, in the meantime, that the Colonel stole up to the bedroom once a day to slice off a piece of the hidden meat. She had kept it to herself up to now. For one thing, she didn't want to ruin the holidays for her husband, and for another, she had to prepare herself for an explanation that was even worse, even more horrible than her surprise, her uncertainty.

It was cool here, Lucienne remarked, and then she began to talk about her son. She sat on one of the beds, sunk in the soft white mountain of the comforter, and Schacht stood at the foot of the bed like a doctor with an incurable case. Memory transfigures things, and how, isn't that so, my dear Schacht? It's a sharp blinding light that frames the deceased and tranforms him into a shadow that disappears.

In mid-January they buried Representative Blocher, car accident, and the wreaths of roses and bright ribbons and bouquets lay in the white landscape like a tropical island. The ground was hard as glass and the glass cracked, the snow became mushy, and Blocher's grave receded behind fresh rows of graves. Time passed over the land, and each day the Colonel and his wife visited their son. In February he caught the flu. He felt feverish, sweaty, had chills, then developed a cough that grew steadily worse, it was a military kind of cough, terse and stiff. Oh, it's nothing, he said to himself, just the price to be paid for a few Havanas I puffed on damp nights in the tent. Lucienne remained at home for two days, demonstratively, it was fine with him, he carried on as usual at the grave, suppressing, however, his desire to call the animal over to him, to stroke her coat, scratch her neck. He laughed at the doctor. The air was good for him, he was sure of that. So his wife accompanied him once again, there was no mention of his cough, and when they reached the corner of the chapel, the Colonel made sure to turn his head and glance back over his shoulder, but he spotted her only once—a shadow hurrying down from the top of the wall to disappear behind the granite rock. I hope you enjoy it, my little kitty.

"What are you thinking about?"

She asked this question more and more often, and the Colonel always gave the same answer: Nothing, he wasn't thinking of anything. As he seldom scattered the birdseed, he was always carrying bags full of it around with him, only that day he had added another, and he decided to go to the lake early the next morning and empty his pockets. He hadn't lied, he hated to lie. He really wasn't thinking about anything, but in spite of that something was creeping, sneaking, toward him, a kind of feeling, a kind of desire he could not understand or get rid of, it was something vague, painfully pleasant, and the feeling grew stronger week by week, day by day.

The cat had grown dear to his old and tired heart.

The Colonel committed his fatal mistake in March, and it was a mistake typical of a trooper. He had concentrated all of his forces toward the front, which was justifiable, the situation was critical. The snow had melted and there was no foliage. Would she continue to take the high road? He doubted it. She leapt down from a mound of snow the gardener had shoveled against the wall; it lay in shadow, it was true, but the mound was scarred and cratered, black at the edges, it was getting smaller and dirtier by the day, and at twilight the Colonel could hear the sound of her claws scratching on the ancient wall. She could get up there only with great effort. What should he do? Order more flowers for the Siegenthalers' grave? He stamped back and forth nervously, and almost welcomed his cough. It would cover the sound of the scratching. The temperature was climbing, there was a high-pressure system over the North Atlantic, but the branches looked like iron rods, no, nothing was blooming, nothing, it never would. The gravel path was soft under his boots, mushy at the edges, and his steps made a gurgling sound. The graves were wet, it was a race against time. But then, overnight, spring unfolded like a brightly painted fan, a Japanese watercolor in airy, light strokes. The cherry trees planted above the cemetery were abloom in white, colorful sprays of flowers spilled out of vases placed on the graves, boats sailed past each other in the bight below, and the two Siegenthalers' urns disappeared so suddenly under the jungle roof it was as though fleshy plants had parachuted down and landed on the neighboring graves—the cat moved along under this, concealed from above, the danger had passed. It no longer made sense, the Colonel noted in passing, to continue feeding the birds.

"Yes, dear," Lucienne called, and then, looking up from gathering twigs, she said: "There's that scratching sound again, what's that strange scratching sound?"

"It's me," the Colonel answered.

He'd been at work for some days now on the cemetery wall. He was scraping off the loose mortar to spackle the joints.

"You and your ideas!" Lucienne called. Then she bundled the twigs and carried them to the container.

Yes, the Colonel had thought of everything, of the scratching sound her claws made and how to cover it; of the possibility that she would appear in the open and what he would do about it; he had overlooked only one thing: his daughters' bedroom was aired and cleaned every spring.

For the whole winter, for almost half a year, everything had gone without a hitch. When he knew she was at the stove, or in the bathroom, he hurried to the bedroom to retrieve the necessary ration. He would wrap it in his handkerchief and put it in the pocket of his house jacket. He told Lucienne that the doctor had advised him to wear his jacket underneath his officer's coat to protect him from the wind and weather.

He was still lying in bed when a scream split the air. At that moment he knew—the cleaning woman! He had forgotten the cleaning woman, his base camp had been discovered.

Well, it was the plain truth: he had stored up emergency rations, and because Lucienne never asked him for whom or to what purpose, it had never been necessary for him to lie.

How does disaster begin? And is it possible that its smile is pure mask? If you rip away the first layer, the second appears, the empty mouth becomes a grin, the eye sockets stare, and the Colonel thought he already knew what he would see behind the final disguise.

His base camp had been discovered, a new one had to be set up, and actually it got off to a good start. But that too appeared to be part of the game—we're supposed to meet the false countenance with a smile, cheerfully blinded.

It happened thus: He had gone to his desk in an ill humor, and sullenly had removed old files from long-unused drawers, papers, his tools, his drawing compass, his compass, calculator and— whether it was the whiskey or the fact that his trusted instruments and message forms invoked the spirit of his successes—his mood improved.

He leafed through the papers, he dreamed, he read.

And suddenly the sun, and the icy snow of Alpine glaciers, shone between the lines of his transcribed orders; a command to establish a howitzer position in the mountains evoked memories; he heard the names of comrades long dead called out in loud voices, voices that brought alive before his eyes troop movements, successful maneuvers, and the smoky atmosphere of bygone nights spent in tents. Light streaming warm and golden through the window of a farm into the blue gloom of a winter night; stunted trees—the last outposts before the mountain wilderness be-

gan—stood ancient and alert above the slumber-
ing lowland; the white line of a river or a road
snaked through the valley that lay in the shadow
of high cliffs; nearby the falls roared down, foaming, into the depths, and the Colonel climbed up
farther, higher, the roar became a murmur, a
sing-song, it faded, died away, and now, far from
those he loved, high above the abyss, he walked
into the silence, into the high, bright light of a
mountain day.

He worked and dreamed deep into the night.

He opened another bottle and finished writ-
ing, in a strongly disguised hand, a love letter to
Elvira Fonti, the wife of his former division commander. "I kiss you, my beloved, and anxiously
look forward to seeing you, Your Long-Secret
and Unknown Admirer. P.S.: I suggest you
bring along your friend Lucienne, with whom I
am acquainted, as chaperone. I would think the
old girl would understand, and it would satisfy
convention. I am counting on you, Cordially
Yours."

He posted the letter that same night. The
following day Lucienne, obviously upset, told
him that Elvira, her best friend, had urgently
requested a visit from her, alert phase one,
yes, now, right away. He was surprised. The
unknown admirer had set the rendezvous for

the day after tomorrow, but apparently Elvira
wished to discuss what she would wear. "So go,"
he growled, "and give the old dragon my best."

Lucienne did not return until late that evening, leaning on Zizi's arm, the daughter as pale
as her mother, obviously they were both suffering from the föhn, the warm, dry south wind of
spring, or from a migraine caused by it, they
didn't give him a glance. Had something gone
wrong? Tuesday morning he knew for sure:
everything was all right. Lucienne gave him a
kiss good-bye. She didn't say where she was
going, but the Colonel was convinced that she
would head right for Elvira's side at the Ascot
Café, where her unknown admirer wished, between the hours of two and four that afternoon,
to hand the woman of his dreams a rose.

At the stroke of four the Colonel had con-
cluded his work, the new base camp was established. When Lucienne arrived home a while
later, he was sitting in his chair with the plaid
blanket wrapped around his legs, his mouth open
and his eys shut. Lucienne, he could tell, stood
for a long time in the doorway. Then she touched
him lightly on the head, wake up, mon cher, it's
time to go to the cemetery.

And so a second unfortunate incident followed closely on the heels of the first. The Colo-

nel, by mistake, had put the fake love letter in
an envelope clearly printed on the back with his
name, rank, and regiment.

And yet, he told himself, and yet, he had
succeeded in getting Lucienne out of the house
for two hours and in stowing the goods in a new,
secure place. Didn't that count more than the
humiliation? Wasn't that more important than the
gossip about him that was circulating in the barracks, the giggling of the officers' widows, the
grins of his sons-in-law?

It was no longer to be denied, it could no longer
be suppressed: her husband had lost his mind.
Lucienne stood in the hall. The ticking of the
parlor clock could be heard through the walls, it
creaked, then chimed, it was eleven o'clock at
night.

She jumped. The stags! There they were
again, just as when her son lay dying—the herd
had awakened, had come to life, ready to leap.

Her father had shot the stags decades before,
in the Carpathian Mountains supposedly. Hunting trophies, he had said, are not animals, are not
pictures. She had been too small at the time to
understand the grand old man, but had compre-

hended that he bestowed a magical power on the heads and antlers. They jutted out from the wall of the entry hall, high above the heads of the house's occupants and visitors, a panoramic garland that for years had proclaimed the hunter's prowess. It was true that on the evening he moved in, the Colonel, as new master of the house, had declared that he was interested neither in hunting nor in the chase, but he was obliged, of course, to let his wife decide. So the trophies remained where they were, the single reminder of her father. They were forgotten in time, accumulated dust, their eyes clouded over, their snouts aged. But cracks were appearing at the neatly severed necks, star shapes thin as spider webs, and if she looked at them closely the dust was no longer dust, their eyes were not blind, and their snowy snouts were sniffing the hall air. It smelled like snow, like the forest. This deathly quiet! That was how it had been as their son lay dying, and that was how it was now, living alone in this huge ship of a house with the crazy Colonel—the deathly quiet appeared to remind the herd of its winter forests, and was luring them back to life. From the top floor she could hear the patter of naked feet, and later the loud, menacing roar of the toilet flushing, and whether the primordial snout of a fallow buck, brought down decades before, had actually moved, or whether the power of Lucienne's imagination had temporarily overwhelmed her—the old buck solved the riddle with his grinding jaw. He was her husband, she was fond of him, but her true love, the great and burning love of her life, had passed through him to her son, her dead son. He must have felt that. It hurt him. He wasn't used to that, he wouldn't stand for it, and for that reason and that reason alone the man was contriving all sorts of things to reclaim his original place in her feelings. If only she had taken him at his word! Emergency rations! Of course—he wanted to demonstrate how concerned he was, day and night, for the family's survival. In the case of mobilization they would be supplied with meat for a while, whole cabinets full of meat, you see, I've taken care of it, I, the Captain. Even his letter to Elvira, with its roguish request to have her, Lucienne, come along as chaperone, could easily be explained—it was she, his own wife, whom he was courting and wanted to win back. And that was the reason, the sole reason, that he visited the grave daily, despite his cough, despite his fever: he wanted to force her love. I too, he silently tried to make clear evening after evening, am sad, as sad as you, our feelings are the same, we are close to one another, closer than ever before.

A sentence was uttered from the wall, the utterance of a dead animal—Lucienne understood it immediately: I am your stag, I am your master. He was jealous of her grief. He would not tolerate sharing her with anyone, not even with the son he had survived. That was the stag's message, and Lucienne, as if she were still a small girl in a sailor suit, giggled a little and thanked it with a curtsey. She proceeded as carefully as if she were walking on ice and, in the sparkling stars of the chandelier's crystal prisms, she turned off the light and slipped quickly out of her shoes. Then she climbed the stairs along the dark windows, to the attic. She stood on the roof for a while every evening. But no one knew that, not even Zizi, her confidante.

Lucienne pushed open the skylight and stepped out—into the sky, into the night.

For a while everything took its usual course. Every few weeks right before dawn, the Colonel anticipated the appearance of Lance-Corporal Habernoll at their appointed meeting place. He was as punctual as the cat, he was aware of what he owed his former commander. Though the road was flat he marched out of the twilight leaning forward like a Swiss infantryman from the

mountains, small, old, and slow, and walked
along the Meier-Labiche industrial complex,
crossed the embankment looking neither to the
right nor the left, then crossed Canton Strasse,
and only when he reached the Colonel, who was
waiting for him, did he straighten his back and
let the rucksack slide down his leg to the ground.
"Lance-Corporal Habernoll, Colonel, with the
provisions."

"Thank you, Lance-Corporal, how are
things?"

"Last week a cat had kittens. She ate two of
them herself, I took care of the rest."

The man then collected his fee for butchering
and delivery, swung over his shoulder the empty
sack the Colonel brought with him each time,
stood at attention, then bent over again and
marched off back home to the mountains, as
stooped as he had been when he arrived. The
meat he had brought with him was then smuggled to the cemetery in small portions and buried
in the earth around the grave. Yes, everything
was taking its course. They went to the cemetery,
it had turned summer, it was hot, the earth had
dried up, and the Colonel conserved his waning
strength. When the distance to the bench in front
of the chapel became too far for him to walk, he
sat down behind the granite rock—the stone, he

said, was cool, it did him good. Lucienne was watering the flowers. "I see what you're up to," she called, laughing, "you're afraid one of your soldiers might catch you doing grave and gardening work."

He sat in the shadows, he was tired and said nothing.

"I know you, mon cher, you are more vain than you imagine!"

Why the devil did she use the word "imagine"? Did she imagine something? Suddenly he sat up. He wanted to scream. He was terribly angry, wild with fury. What do you mean? Do you really believe that I am ashamed of our work here? That I would be capable—I, the commander—of hiding from a subordinate? But the Colonel said nothing. Empathetic and sensitive as she was, she had tried to find a halfway decent explanation for his crouching in the shadows. She wanted to prevent her husband from feeling ashamed in front of his wife. And as quickly as his anger had flared up, it died down again. Everything up here turned out all right. This was the front, the soldier was in his element here. What was it that Zollikofer had said? Never make a needless move. Learn to hesitate, to wait. Note it for life, gentlemen of the general staff—if you have nothing to do, do it right away! Loud laugh-

ter and applause. That was Zollikofer. He knew
how to engrave certain key phrases in their brains
in a way that made them unforgettable, with
pithy military humor—years later, finding themselves in battle, under attack or in retreat, what
now, what shoud they do, and then they would
remember the old man just in time: Gentlemen,
we wait. We let them come, open a pincer, then
attack. Lucienne walked to the fountain with her
empty watering can and the Colonel buried supplies for his cat in the parched earth.

It was magnificent, the big storm in early August,
at least at the beginning!
   An angry black cloud cover appeared over the
crest of the hill; the willows waved, the gardeners' aprons fluttered, leaves and blossoms twisted
in the wind, were tossed into the air and blown
away, and then, suddenly, the first clap of thunder. A roar over the city and the bight, an explosion, and for a fraction of a second everything
shattered, the graves and the gravestones, the
holy-water fonts, vases, crucifixes, wreaths,
urns. The thunderclap was sudden, the brightness
was sudden, and the first drops were already falling, a flood, a torrent, he grabbed her hand, heard
her calling, yelling, but from behind him as if
from a distance. He pulled her along with him,

stumbling, over the graves, across the paths, through the bushes and into the funeral chapel, where they finally stopped, laughing, soaked with rain, wheezing, happy. Outside the sky poured down glistening streams of light and water, thunder boomed, sirens wailed, but they were safe here, they had escaped the storm. A lamp burned dimly. It smelled of candles, faded flowers, of death. There was a body lying in a coffin on the bier. The corpse's bony hands were crossed below its chin, it wore a waxy mask, its eyes were held closed with adhesive. It was humid and still, yet cool, and outside, life bubbled, sprayed and gurgled and pattered, her chest rose and fell, her face was shiny with rain and sweat, he kissed her on the mouth. They sat on the floor against the wall. There were no benches here, only the dead man in the coffin in the middle of the room had a seat. He laid his head on her breast. He was happy to be able to give her a sign of his reawakened feelings, paralyzed by his long period of mourning, he put his hand between her thighs and suddenly he felt her tongue on his throat. Lucienne was licking away the moisture, rain or sweat or both, then he had to cough, just a little, but as concerned about him as she was, his little phenol mouse quickly reached into his jacket pocket, taking out his handkerchief, and with it, twisted into it as always, the meat. "What is this?"

Then she said nothing further, she wept. Meat. Once again she had discovered meat, as in the bedroom, raw, bloody meat. And he, calmness personified, ate it, the entire clump, meat from Lance-Corporal Habernoll, maybe pork, maybe even a dead dog, and he choked on it, but the Colonel forced the meat down his throat to his stomach. "You know," he said finally, "there's something wrong with my appetite."

The body laid out before them, the humming of the air-conditioner coming up through the floor, the lightly trembling concrete, and outside the storm became a murmur in the evening.

"I always carry a little something with me in my pocket," he added. "An old soldier's rule. Eat when you're hungry."

Now he had to cough.

"Eat," he said, "when there's a break in the fighting. Zollikofer. That's what Zollikofer said."

And wants to talk about Zollikofer, but he can't talk, he has to crawl to the door on all fours and tries to open it, hanging onto the handle, and then he doubles over—vomits on the doorsill. When they finally walk out into the open, the storm is receding, a cloud bank with long beards that rake against the distant mountains in the fresh blue light of evening. He gives her his arm. He leads her to the east gate, opens it, and lets her pass through. There is an inscription engraved in the arch above the gate: WHAT YOU ARE, WE WERE. WHAT WE ARE, YOU SHALL BECOME.

Where was their daughter? Then they see the tree lying across the road, it was impossible for cars to get through, his knees feel like jelly. Just don't collapse now, the Colonel orders himself.

IV

One evening when it was still winter Lucienne heard a soft meowing at the cemetery, it was a cat apparently. The Colonel,
however, went ashen, as if she had caught him
doing something monstrous. His eyes opened
wide, his hands shook, and then, only a few
weeks later, in March or April—it was spring at
any rate, the air was already mild—there was the
sound of claws scratching the wall, it was this
cat again, and again he had a look of panic, of
horror. Then he managed to stage a coughing

fit, he was obviously trying to cover the sound,
she wasn't meant to hear the animal. But why?
At that point she hadn't been able to explain his
behavior to herself. Yet another quirk, she
thought, who cares.

Since the evening of the storm, in the chapel,
Lucienne had known that the stag's message had
been wrong—false, basically—and she almost felt
it a mockery that the day that had opened her
eyes had arrived with such force, with thunder
and lightning. Her pain was great, so great that
for days she could not feel it at all. She moved
through the rooms of the house like a sleep-
walker, like some absent-minded person who is
looking for something and in the course of the
search forgets what she is looking for. Sometimes
the furniture wavered before her eyes, became
draped in a damp shroud, and only then would
she realize that her eyes were filled with tears.
She felt deceived, and at the same time misused.
It had become increasingly necessary for her to
support the sickly old man on her arm in order
for him to reach the back of the gravestone
where, as she had noticed in the meantime, he
buried a piece of meat every day—meat, in the
earth where her dead son was buried! That was
more than betrayal. He had feigned grief, carried
his golf bag for her, won back her love, but in
truth and in his actions he had made his wife an

unwitting accomplice to his perverse activities. Out of revenge? Was this cat his answer to the slab of granite? Had he still not come to terms with the fact that it was a stone that stood at the grave and not a rosebush? Her bloodshot eyes looked back at her from her bathroom mirror, and these eyes were the only thing that was alive in the old woman's forlorn face. Swollen tear ducts. Furrows, wrinkles, slack breasts. Should she try to talk to him? She looked at the pills in the palm of her hand, tossed them into her mouth, and prayed that a terrible fight would take place that very night, a decisive battle of angry words, the end of their marriage. Then from her eyes came a moist and moving beam of light, and the woman who had been prepared for battle the moment before began to dissolve in the mirror, she was crying again. An evil God had wrenched her son from her, and now a cemetery cat was stealing her husband. Her heart hardened. There were no longer any men in Lucienne's life, at least none who were alive, and it was just this time of the year, when nature was undergoing its great transformation, reminding old people of the transience of time, that the dead grew in power—like black birds of the night they swept through Lucienne's thoughts and dreams, with a cat in their claws that perished high above the earth. It was six in the morning. She called her eldest daughter, and later that morning she drove with Zizi to Zurich. Lucienne bought herself a brightly colored hat on Bahnhof Strasse, and had her hair done in the latest style.

"What's the matter?" Zizi asked.

"Nothing," said Lucienne. Only a cat. A cemetery cat. And then it erupted, everything erupted. She was furious, a rush of blood shot from her stomach up her back to her brain so suddenly, so forcefully that it took her breath away right there on the street. She was furious at Zizi. Yes, at Zizi and her stupid Toyota. Papa, she had said, is no longer so young. Be a dear and pick us up. It's too long a way for his old feet to carry him, look how he's suffering, how his grief is eating away at him! And her daughter, dumb as she was, obeyed. Showed up at the east gate in that god-awful ugly Toyota evening after evening to take the old man back home. Voluntarily. Without complaint. Duty-bound. And didn't notice how she was being manipulated, used, sapped daily. For the cat! Yes, my child, that's the way it is, that's the truth—without your help he would have surrendered long ago, old and weak as he is. Lucienne gasped for air. "Could I ask you something, my dear?"

Zizi nodded, smiling. She appeared to be enjoying the excursion with her mother.

"When will you finally grow up?"

Zizi was still smiling.

"On top of which—" Lucienne screamed, "why does it have to be a Toyota? Why a Japanese car? Haven't you noticed that the Japs are taking over the world?"

"Mama," Zizi stammered, "je t'en prie—"

"Mama! Mama! Stop it. It's nauseating. Yes, my dear, you're well on your way to becoming a governess to your unhappy parents. But we don't need that, Papa and I, we don't want it, we're still strong enough to stand on our own feet. It's time for you to get yourself pregnant. Or adopt a child. You can get one in the Third World cheap. They're just waiting to be claimed by frustrated psycho-corpses from the West and pumped full of all kinds of neuroses. Oh, I can't go on," Lucienne stammered, "forgive me, my dear. I beg of you, forgive me."

Zizi pushed a strand of hair behind one ear. She was incapable at that point of responding to her mother's outburst with so much as a feeling, much less a thought.

"Shall we have something to eat?" Lucienne asked. "My treat."

A few days after the big storm was the first anniversary of the day the Colonel had started feed-

ing the cat, and in September, which was dreary
and cool that year, he began to feel that he was
not going to survive the coming winter. The
situation was serious, hopeless actually, for he
had to attend to his daily responsibility as before,
observing all kinds of precautions just as if nothing at all had happened. He refilled his glass. His
cat wanted to live, simply to hunt and eat and
live. That was the gist of it, the essence, nothing
else mattered. Whether she was aware of it or
not, his age—the important thing was to carry
on. Who said anything about victory, survival
was everything. Duty. A soldier's way. Flags
flying, upright, resolute to the end. He would
protect the animal. What was it that Napoleon
had said? It had been after the battle of the Berezina River, they had snow up to their hips, farm-
steads were burning to ashes under the red sky.
A Swiss regiment had covered him in retreat,
forming a hollow square as if on a parade ground,
and had faced the advancing Russians, coura-
geous to the end, fire, reload, fire: until no one
was left standing, gentlemen, not one single soldier, and Napoleon said to his marshals: Never
tangle with the Swiss, they're created for defense,
and yes, the Colonel said to himself, the cat shall
be defended, we won't give up so quickly, let
Ivan attack, fire, reload, fire: We'll stand until we
fall.

He had slipped out of his chair without noticing, his glass in his right hand. Her floor lamp was on. A new hairdo? he would like to have asked, the old girl had fixed herself up, good, but he wasn't able to talk to his wife, who was sitting rigidly at her desk, he leaned his head back against the seat of his chair and looked at the ceiling. We can choose neither the time nor the place of battle—we are summoned, and then we must prove ourselves wherever we are, some on the Berezina, others at Monte Cassino, he himself at the grave of his son. Who said anything about victory, survival is everything.

They never mentioned the storm again, so he had no idea whether she had guessed his secret or not. Nevertheless, the Colonel got the feeling that his wife could spend the long evenings with him only with effort. She sat there stiffly, silent as a stone.

"What are you thinking about?"

She seemed not to have heard his question. He staggered over to the radio, turned the dial to some sort of Algerian singsong, and Lucienne, her album pressed to her breast, left the room without a word. He grinned. Though they were old and had lived long enough, the Colonel thought, they would muster some final strength and strangle each other in an embrace.

"Good night, Lucienne!" he called out into

the hall, but there was no answer from upstairs.

He was called Casac in the family jargon, just as he had been called in the army, a Catholic sacramentarian—the Protestant version was Prosac, the difference being that with the Casac, the troop's beloved field priest, you met in private. He had been her husband's staff chaplain, had baptized all of their children, presided over their daughters' marriages, and buried their son. Lucienne liked the Casac. She was scarcely bothered by his penchant for drink, which began early each morning with the communion cup. When he came to visit he would throw himself onto the sofa, lean back his head, and blow cigar smoke in a straight line up to the ceiling. In this pose, as her friend Elvira had commented decades ago, he resembled the great poet Gottfried Benn. He didn't have a skull, he had the noble head of a poet. He had published a book, actually, in 1939: sermons against the advancing enemy. Hitler's soldiers were depicted as scoundrels, beer-bellied flunkies and hounds from hell that had been let off their leashes, so that it was not a sin, but rather one's most sacred patriotic duty to plunge a Swiss bayonet into the enemy's barbarian blood and to sentence those damned assassins and butchers to death and destruction for their deeds. But the barbarians had not attacked after all, and follow-

ing the war the Casac had restricted his poetic
temperament to melancholic aperçus that appeared from time to time in the army newspaper:
"Love life and laugh, my friends, for you never
know when the bell will toll for you." Or, more
to the point: "Life is too short to drink bad wine."
He was also considered to be a highly gifted, if
somewhat risqué, funeral orator, no longer quite
with the times, but the men and women who
listened to him were getting older each year, they
didn't mind his platitudes. Which of us will be
next, they would ask themselves, and look
around at the group gathered at the grave. One
by one they withdrew to the hospitals, the old
age homes, the grave, and by the time their son
was buried the list of those absent was longer
than those who attended. The Casac had written
the Colonel's funeral sermon years ago, he said,
and put it in a drawer, with only the cause of
death to be added.

When the *Laetitia*'s study echoed with his
laughter it made the crystal in the glass cabinet
tinkle, and it seemed to Lucienne that the Casac's
laugh was almost the only thing in their circle
that had remained fresh and cocky. The old comrades and their wives, insofar as they still showed
up, were no longer capable of coming up with
anything even remotely animated, they were

brittle, like glass, and Elvira Fonti hid her ill-fitting dentures, which crunched when she grinned, behind a hand that was covered with liver spots.

As opposed to the Colonel, who was totally fixated on the United States in regard to military matters, the Casac revered Rommel and Mont-gomery. "I personally," he said from time to time, "prefer the trooper to the strategist, and you see, my dear, good old Monty was both a strategist and a trooper, and he was perfect as both. When Monty visited this country, he even inspected the woodpiles—a true gentleman!" And the Casac would laugh again, give his ring-ing laugh and reach for his glass, to drain it in one swallow. It was truly a wonder, thought Lucienne, that the old boy was able to conduct Mass without breaking out laughing.

Previously he had appeared like clockwork every Thursday afternoon for tea, though he hated with a passion everything concerning time and its passing. "But really," he had said at Zizi's wedding celebration—Lucienne's gift to the bride had been a hand-carved Black Forest clock—"but really, what do we need clocks for, our time will pass soon enough on its own." And she had agreed with his mockery, a bit piqued. He was right, their eldest was now married and the others were soon to follow, what do we need clocks for, our time will pass soon enough on its own. Yes, that was typical Casac—he detested clocks and was punctual to a fault. When the clock struck three, he would be standing there in the hall, then he would throw himself onto the sofa and start to laugh. Why? No one knew. Perhaps he saw a fly and found it funny that flies crawled around on ceilings.

My dear Casac—she would begin like that. You know how precious my husband is to me, he is the father of my children. I could have forgiven him anything, believe me, but this animal—no. I simply cannot forgive that.

Then he would look up inquisitively. How's that, dear friend, did I hear you correctly—an animal?

Yes, my dear, oh yes, and it took even me a long time to figure it out. My husband submits his emotions, you know, to the same logical process as he does his thinking. He hates uncertainty in any form, including the spiritual. In any given situation he will reach for the dissecting knife of his logic, to give his emotions a good going over and classify them correctly into categories. Staff work, if you know what I mean. Careful planning and subsequent execution, in bed as well, everywhere, really, that's Zollikofer's style, Zollikofer taught him how to live.

Good old Zolli!

True, she would answer quickly, in order not
to give the Casac any opportunity to launch into
the flattering funeral oration he had delivered for
Zollikofer, true, my dear Captain, but grief, you
see, is an oddly mixed drink. Memory is blended
in—happiness, that is to say. And longing, a
pleasant homesick feeling, a sweet sorrow. And
equal portions of despair, which bubbles up in
the throat, and discord, and rage, that's right,
rage at the Creator as well, a vengeful blasphemy.
Our son is dead and we are alive. Are you following me, Captain? Grief is a strange experience, the essence of life, so to speak. Everything
gets jumbled. Pain and happiness become one and
the same. And yet not the same, but why am I
telling you this, you know exactly what I'm talking about. An intellect shaped by Zollikofer isn't
trained to handle grief. It breaks down. Breaks
down in a terrible way. For grief is a volcano, and
what bubbles up out of this realm of the spirits
and the dead—it was an all-consuming fog in my
husband's case. Night. Confusion. And what
does the good man do? You won't believe it,
Captain—he lures a cat to the cemetery and feeds
it.

How's that?

A cat, yes, that's right, but the worst of it
is—he feeds it behind my back. And that, I am
sorry to say, is treason, betrayal, a cruel insult to

those feelings I hold most sacred. Along with the
summerhouse, Captain, my grief for my son is
the most valuable thing I possess. I would go
even further. It is only in this summerhouse,
which I no longer set foot in, by the way, and
in my grief that I am able to recognize myself.
It is only there that a part of me is still alive, a
pathetic part, the quivering shadow of a once-
happy Lucienne.

Or something to that effect. She needed the
Casac then as never before. But after her son died,
the field priest canceled his visits, just as Elvira
Fonti had, and on Thursday afternoons Lucienne
and the Colonel sat in their chairs, drank their
tea, and waited for guests who never came.

They had been taking a taxi to the cemetery
since the weather had gotten cooler, and their
daughter drove them back home in her Toyota.
Lucienne looked forward to All Souls' Day. The
entire family would gather for Mass and a visit
to the graveside, and the *Laetitia*, rolling on its
bank like a scrapped vessel this time of the year,
would come to life.

It smelled like tar, like train stations and depar-
ture. She stood for a while on the roof, as she
had on that previous evening, the myriad white

beds far beneath her, all covered in cloth. She had daydreamed up here as a child; as a mother she had come here to rest from her children, alone at last, far from her daughters' chatter; and now that the *Laetitia* was empty she felt a happiness here, under her feet the past came alive—the warmth that rose from the battlement became the breath of her sleeping children. The breeze barely grazed the treetops in the park, stars shone in the night sky, the lake had a veneer of black varnish.

Then she heard the Colonel open the door to the terrace, go down the steps, and cross the gravel, he was going out into the park, into the dead of night.

Lucienne stepped back from the landing, her heel struck a deck chair, its rods were rotten, its canvas faded by the elements. It was time, she thought, for someone to straighten up things up here. But she thought that every evening, and she knew that the deck chairs would remain here, flotsam from better days. Her daughters had sunned themselves in them years ago, and for a while a rumor had circulated among the squadron commanders of the air force that Debrunner, the Mirage pilot, had succeeded one May morning in capturing the Colonel's daughters in a suggestive aerial photo.

The Colonel had disappeared among the trees. Was it coincidence that he had begun taking nightly walks right after the Elvira Fonti affair? Coincidence or not, ever since then he had left the house at the same time each evening—he had business in the park. Business, that was the right word, for he crept off so punctually, so regularly, almost like a bookkeeper, that she could not help guessing that his new meat reserve was in the summerhouse. The summerhouse, of all places! Well, during the summer she had tolerated his nocturnal walks, they couldn't harm his health, but now it was October, the temperature had dropped, sooner or later, she knew, she would have to act.

To the north, MEIER-LABICHE had written his name in neon in the night sky and the great complex, which during the day was veiled in the smoke that poured from its chimneys, grew huge in the night and gave off a cold glow. As if a machine of iron and glass were exploding in slow motion, chimneys sprouted, roofs welled up, workshops glowed from within, and windows and chalky white concrete surfaces were lit by high beams of light. Meier-Labiche had once belonged to those guests who were invited to the *Laetitia* on appointed days, and the major holidays as well.

She once again stood on the landing that was crusted with rust, and looked down into the darkness. She began to discern things in the gloom that surrounded the summerhouse—a branch appeared out of the black shadows, a trunk, and a pale circle betrayed the eaves of the tin dome. The Colonel apparently had turned on a light inside, a flashlight or petroleum lamp. Tears ran down her cheeks. The summerhouse was the thing most sacred to her, the memory of her happiest times.

It was his fault. He must have known what he was doing. She would not tolerate the summerhouse becoming some sort of icebox for his meat supply. Tomorrow, Lucienne swore to herself, tomorrow she would act.

When she came out of anesthesia her daughters were gathered around the bed with bouquets of flowers, they were strangely silent, motionless, a waxworks. Someone was holding her hand, someone said sadly and softly: She's dying.

She had sat bolt upright in the middle of the night. The Colonel was sitting on the bed, and the sentence she then uttered later became a family adage: "You smell like sausage," Lucienne said.

The next day the Casac performed an emergency baptism. Against all expectation, Lucienne recovered quickly but she stayed in the hospital and sat at the incubator, dressed as a nurse, for long and anxious weeks. The child inside was fighting for his life—a sticky bundle of flesh and blood hooked up to plastic tubes. "Be reasonable," his mother said, "and go home."

"He's my son," the Colonel said, "he can beat death."

He was right. After six months, the child was removed from his glass shrine and taken home to the *Laetitia*. Lucienne ordered flags hung from all masts, garlands on all decks, gala uniforms for the officers and troops—and her son screamed in his mother's arms. He screamed so loudly and so strongly that he threatened to choke on his screams and burst his tiny heart. His mother felt it: He was screaming for the angel. So she climbed up to the attic with her child, laid him down on an old mattress, took the nurse's uniform she had not worn for years out of the trunk, put it on, and set her nurse's cap on her head. When she emerged again from the house, the men were nonplussed. They were still standing on the green and Gerber, the Colonel's former orderly who had taken care of the *Laetitia*'s park since his retirement, did not at first seem to recognize his mistress. They opened a column for her, her daughters to the left, the staff to the right, and her steps crunched so loudly in the gravel that it sounded as though she were walking on popcorn. But her son lay quietly in her arms, he felt at home among nurses—quiet and the white hospital were his world. She carried him into the summerhouse. It was bright inside, there was a faded painting in the dome, and white garden furniture, white window frames. And the sun, flashing through the trees in the park and seeping through the opening at the top of the structure at noon, must have reminded him of the light behind the glass of his incubator. When fall came, Gerber installed an electrical heater, he repaired the cracks and laid rugs down on the wooden floor. Lucienne wore her nurse's uniform and lived in the summerhouse with her son day and night for a full two years—the Colonel had set up his cot there for her.

Lucienne arranged her daughters in casual poses in the armchairs, you hold a book, you take your knitting, I would suggest that you look out the window, but not so melancholy, that would be too much, the two of you can play chess, Zizi will sit at the piano and, oh yes, the little one can sit next to you for a duet. Are we ready?

"A l'attaque, mes belles, les officiers arrivent!"

Schacht led them in. They arrived through the park carrying rubbery red bunches of gladioli that were meant for Lucienne. Voices, laughter, and soon it smelled of aftershave and boot polish and cigar smoke on all decks. They ate and drank and sang, and right before midnight they snaked through the park in a polonaise. Il Capitano and his wife stood on the bridge, that is to say on the terrace balustrade, he with a glass in his right hand, she waving—the *Laetitia*, festively lit, steamed through the summer night. Then il Capitano retired, it got quiet, here and there a waterfowl cried, waves smacked against the quay, and as much as she didn't want to, as reluctant as she was to disturb things—Lucienne had to go look for the boy, he had disappeared. One couple was in a deep embrace in the summerhouse, one in the laundry room, one under the trees, one on the footpath behind the house, in the boathouse, and Zizi, the eldest, was sitting in the study with Schacht, absorbed in the question of whether, in a war fought in the mountains, one could do without mules, independent as they were of the weather and fuel. Schacht was arguing heatedly in favor of the helicopter.

They left only in the gray light of morning. Comrades, Schacht called, end of exercise, about face, march—destination, barracks!

Thus ended the all-night ballet choreographed

by her daughters, who were standing now on the gravel square, their clothes and hair in disarray. The eastern sky took on a salmon-colored light, and Lance-Corporal Gerber rested his head among the empty bottles on the kitchen table, he was asleep. He couldn't stand those men. Gigolos, he always said, they're three-quarters crazy.

During the last months of his life Gerber looked as if he were a brew of skin and bones. He didn't drink anymore, he guzzled. His cancer, he said, needed to swim. It was only seldom now that he would scratch his marks and hearts into the wood of the kitchen table, mostly he looked out through the park at the lake. Gerber was the first to go overboard. His strength waned, his drunkenness increased, and the work he had done in the garden began to go to pieces before his eyes. The bushes were overgrown, reeds sprang up in the beds, and on many a foggy morning, as the birds were screaming in the treetops and the night dew was dripping heavily from the leaves, the *Laetitia*, old, clumsy steamer that it was, seemed to be stranded in the bight of some feverish tropical island surrounded by a primeval forest. But Anni still chopped the vegetables, stayed busy at the stove, rolled out the dough. He wasn't sick, she said, he was a lazy dog. The lance-corporal nodded. Yes, he said, that was true.

Lucienne stood in the door. Serve the tea in his room, she requested, her son wasn't feeling well that day.

One morning she heard him give a speech on gardening that she never forgot. The gardening profession, the old man was saying to himself, was a profession of stooping over. But the gardener, as opposed to the common waiter, never bowed to people, no, he bent down to what was left of paradise. For every garden was an attempt to recreate that first garden called Eden, and it was to that place, and not to some barren eternity, that mankind returned. Consequently, he requested that his grave be properly landscaped. Lucienne and Anni laughed. A few days later his emaciated body was found lying in front of the stove, his fingers clawing the floor—Gerber was clinging to the steep face of a cliff. The maid left him lying there and fled. No one ever found out where she went, but a good year later a brochure arrived at the house—extolling a foot salve concocted by one Gaston Kalbermatten, and it listed a Madame Anni Kalbermatten as his Swiss representative, orders could be placed by phone. *Pas de style*, her daughters said. They were all still single.

Zizi made the best match. Lieutenant Schacht, originally a theology student, had quickly and successfully made his way through officers' schools and special courses, he had a gift for strategy and was good in the field as well, he advanced faster than the others. After marrying the Colonel's daughter, in the uniform of a first lieutenant, he completed the general staff course, and soon thereafter the word in the upper ranks of the Ninth Mountain Division was that Elvira Fonti saw in Schacht the future commander of the division. Everyone was happy. Schacht got his company command, was promoted to captain, and Zizi became pregnant. Grande fiesta, il Capitano ordered, and once again, for the last time, the *Laetitia* sailed out into the night in celebration, filled with light. There were dancers on the bridge, engaged couples in the park, and il Capitano and his wife in the midst of all this lively excitement, quietly content in a blissful fog of champagne. A few days after that, the staff physician held shadowy X-rays against the high windows of the study. Lucienne understood little of the medical explanation, but on the plastic sheet she saw a human skeleton, plainly and clearly lit by the rays of the noonday sun. The Colonel threw himself into his armchair, and sat with his elbows on his knees and his head in his hands.

"He's my son," he murmured.

Is happiness contagious? Their son lay dying, there was no further mention of Zizi's pregnancy, and Captain Schacht, without warning, quit the instruction corps. For no reason, they said. But word was making its way through the latrines that Schacht had had a physical relationship with a staff sergeant, a rumor that disappeared almost without a trace in view of the captain's impeccable record. The sergeant in question, though blond and muscular, was a good family man, and even Zizi said that her husband was not the type for something like that. Nevertheless, Schacht decided it would be best not to attend the funeral or the funeral dinner. It must have been a difficult decision for him to make—he had been fond of the boy, perhaps had even loved him. At any rate, Schacht and the son of the house had spent countless hours together, working, as they said, ceaselessly planning and building. They had created a veritable work of art in the summerhouse, though it remained unfinished, death had thwarted its completion, and Schacht, just like his mother-in-law, most likely never set foot in the summerhouse again.

From a distant tower a clock struck midnight. Down in the park the Colonel was shuffling toward the *Laetitia*. Lucienne waited until he closed the door to his room, then she stepped back in from the roof and for a long time kept her eyes on the attic light switch, a squat button of black enamel. She hesitated to touch the switch and turn off the light. Why is life so horrible, dearest?

Lucienne had decided to poison the cat.

V

Many years ago a young Vietnamese traveled to Paris. On the day of his arrival he went to the Bibliothèque Nationale and explained, in a courteous speech prepared during his long sea voyage, that Western thought had been described to him as a mental cathedral. He, an ignorant Asian, was now standing before this cathedral as a foreigner, but a curious one, with a great desire to get to know the architect. The librarian recommended Aristotle's *Metaphysics*. The young man memorized it, returned to the jungle, and drove the French colonial army out of his country.

The young man's name was Giap, and he was the commander in chief of the Vietcong. After his victory over the French, the United States army, the strongest military force in the world, became his enemy. In the north, where Giap had been operating for years, he could not be defeated. His plan, however, was to push into the south and force the Americans to withdraw. Once again, he went to work in his own way. First he studied the enemy, its way of thinking and feeling. In the process it became clear to him that Saigon headquarters was expecting him to move, was even trying to bait him by holding back its own troops. The Americans wanted to lure the fox out of his hole and destroy him from the air, far from his base of operations in the north.

The Colonel rolled bits of meat in the wet leaves he had found behind a nearby grave. He was tired but happy, he had studied General Giap's advance in back issues of the Swiss army newspaper until dawn, he was imitating his method.

Giap figured that the Americans, as soon as he began his march, would burn away the rain forests and the rice fields along the route of the march—they poisoned the area, they wanted the Vietcong to die of hunger. But Giap was clever, more clever than they thought. He had everything going against him: his troops were suffering from battle fatigue and the enemy controlled the air; the Americans believed that if they cut off Giap's divisions from supplies and support, they could cripple them halfway to their destination and then destroy them, partly from the air, partly on land.

The Colonel stuffed the meat wrapped in leaves into fist-sized holes, spread cellophane wrap over the opening, and covered his supply depot with earth. He was overwhelmed with happiness. "Are you progressing, dear?" he called to his wife.

He felt victorious. The sly Giap held off the Americans for months in order to carry out his lengthy preparations, undermining them in mock battles. So now he asked for the package of snail poison, she handed it to him around the stone, he scattered a few pellets, gathered them back up again, and put them back in the package. "Oh, these snails," he called, "they're a real nuisance."

Lucienne was still hesitating. She hadn't dispensed her poison. Was she afraid that he would begin ranting today too, as he had yesterday at discovering the toxin? A fit of rage was not necessary today, he was armed. Hats off, Comrade General. He knew the enemy's weapons—poison and napalm—and he now knew as well that the soldier was an animal, yes, an animal. Brilliant, thought the Colonel, a brilliant stategist, this Giap. He succeeded in setting up ground camps in the swamps and forests along the line of advance, and the Americans noticed nothing of Giap's movements, nothing at all! For Giap ordered the work to be done at night and by the civilian population, for the most part. He took his time, he built one camp after the other, and only when the supply chain was completed did he give orders for the long march—destination Saigon. As champagne was flowing in the American high command, Giap crawled out of his hole. Let him come, they laughed. And come he did, cunning little Giap. And the rain forests burned, the rice fields were destroyed, they poisoned the waters in the course of one night. His defeat was a matter of time, the country was decimated, communication was cut off from the rear, bombs fell day and night, the world burned. And Giap's divisions kept marching. Not to win—they marched to eat. They ate their way from one ground camp to the next, ate away their line of withdrawal, and the next supply of rations—always in front them, buried in the swampy jungle soil safe from fire and poison—lured them ever faster toward the south. They overran the enemy positions, but it wasn't out of an eagerness to kill, it wasn't their will to victory or their desire to rush into the jaws of death, this was no crusade against the Western world: It was hunger that drove them, and thirst; they wanted to reach the feeding stations, they wanted to drink water and eat rice, they wanted to live, merely to drink and eat and live. That is how General Giap, with war-weary troops, conquered South Vietnam. The Americans fled in panic, they just left everything lying there, they had to pluck their people from the roofs with helicopters—that was how quickly Giap advanced, that was how fast he took the city. The Colonel stood up, took his flask from his pocket, and allowed himself one last strong drink. They underestimate us at their own risk, he said to himself, and grinned in the blue evening light and offered his wife his arm.

"Do you need the poison to clean the stone?" he asked.

"Let's go," Lucienne said.

Zizi was waiting for them at the east gate.

"How good you look," his wife said to their daughter, "wonderfully, wonderfully well!"

That night he fought his way through the rain forest, it was the rainy season, the fleshy leaves glistened with rain, the trunks dripped water and the ground was swampy, mucky, muddy, so that the Colonel could barely advance into battle. His footsteps gurgled, he was getting nowhere, and decay hung like a rope bridge spanning the jungle high over the void, a soaking-wet, soft-as-butter, chasm-spanning carpet of decay that he sank into, fell into. He lay now in bed, he lay in bed awake, drenched in sweat, exhausted by the dream, but strange, it continued to rain. Was he mistaken?

The rain continued.

The Colonel, who seldom dreamed, now discovered that his nights were more real, more lurid, larger than the days they followed. Lucienne brought him a pot of tea around ten, he got up at noon, they went to the cemetery in the afternoon, their daughter picked them up. On Thursday afternoon at exactly three o'clock, the Casac appeared. Lucienne was visibly glad to see him; the Colonel had requested that the priest come.

"Here's the book," he said.

"Oh, have you brought us something, dear Captain?" Lucienne asked.

It was Aristotle's *Metaphysics*.

Work was out of the question now. Mostly, he stood beside his wife and silently held the umbrella—it was pouring. But despite this, the Colonel carried out his responsibility. It seemed especially easy to do, it was almost miraculous, for every evening, after a moment of silence, his wife left the grave, left him there alone. Each time for a different reason: once, she wanted to visit with a major's widow, another time she had to speak to a gardener, and two or three times the Toyota horn had sounded earlier than usual. That was fine with him. He quickly slipped behind the gravestone and buried the daily ration. It was about the size of an apple and was wrapped in leaves and cellophane. It would have been dangerous for him to prepare the complicated concoction at the grave, so he readied the apple the night before, in the summerhouse where he kept his basic supplies. Then he wrapped it in his handkerchief and put it in his jacket pocket.

The rain continued.

One afternoon Lucienne dug out two yellow sailing jackets, brought two pairs of boots from the basement. The Colonel thanked her, smiling. "Attention! Prepare for rain," he ordered, "we march at the usual time!"

They were alone at the cemetery. The gardeners were huddled in the chapel, slapping jass cards down on the table and drinking schnapps, cursing and laughing. The candles had gone out, only the lanterns still gave off a ragged flame, flowers

97

were bobbing in their flooded vases, and the trash container had become a foul-smelling lagoon; huge water lilies—wilted wreaths—floated there. The small strip between the back of the grave-stone and the cemetery wall had turned into a swamp that had almost become a river, and the Colonel asked himself if his cat, proud of her clean coat, would crawl through this dreck to collect her package. He thought about it for a long time. But he stuck the apple down into the earth anyway. Gentlemen, Zollikofer had in-structed his general staff years before, the worse the weather the greater the possibility of gaining an advantage under the prevailing conditions. That was true. Giap too had taken advantage of the rainy season, and the Colonel observed his wife's worried look with a delight that threatened to turn into a grin. The poor woman would have to wait. Yes, Lucienne was in the same situation as General Westmoreland, Giap's adversary. His planes were grounded in the monsoon season, and her green bottle of poison was sitting on the kitchen table, there was no question of using it in this weather. As a result, it was no longer necessary to pack the meat in leaves and cello-phane, that was true, but the Colonel did just the opposite. He used the rainy season to acclimate his cat to the new situation. For one thing was certain: The poison would be a shock to her, would upset her, it was chemical warfare, assault by poison. It was damned important, he thought, that when D day came she would have only to struggle with the new ground conditions, she already would have learned to tear the meat from its package. She learned quickly. She appeared to have no trouble locating the apple in the mud and getting to her food as before. The Colonel was proud of himself. In these gray, rainy days before All Souls' he proved to himself that he hadn't gotten rusty, wasn't senile, that he was still able to learn, and was as nimble-minded as Giap, and clever as the cat. Without so much as batting an eye he had jettisoned a military ideology he had believed in since the Allies landed at Normandy. The Colonel had rejected the idea of hiding the bottle of poison, or substituting for it something harmless.

Constant rain. He had strange dreams, he slept badly, but he never lost his feeling of happiness. Four days before All Souls', he was stranded with a mechanized division in the Russian mud, the panzer tracks rattled and snapped, they were stuck, they flooded. Cease fire, said Gerber.

He crouched beneath the dripping straw roof of a hut and looked out into the endless expanse of Russia. A sulfur-yellow jellyfish swam across the horizon, it was the sun, and shortly after dawn it began to snow.

Gentlemen, the Russian winter!

Even out here in the Donets Basin, Zollikofer somehow had managed to scrape together chalk and a blackboard. He quickly sketched a child's version of a snowman, wrote the word "Ivan" below it, underlined it twice. An exclamation point, and then, without a sound, straight as a board, he sank into the Russian earth.

The Colonel wept. He was convinced that he had seen Zollikofer for the last time. When he awoke, it was quiet. Water, glinting in the thin morning sun, dripped now only from the rain gutters. It was possible, he thought, that he himself had coughed out the puff of exhaust his tank motor gave off. He threw off his blanket and climbed out of bed. The skin on his legs was cheesy, his leg muscles were slack.

"Last night we were in Russia," he said. "Zollikofer was there too, his number was up."

"Well, well," Lucienne murmured, "well, well."

Interesting, she added, her lips on the paper-thin rim of her porcelain cup, her eyes darting back and forth from the Colonel to the window, from the window to the clock, from the clock to the table.

"It was a dream," the Colonel said.

"Of course it was a dream," said Lucienne.

Lucienne pulled the plastic gloves up to her elbows—it was D day, this was war. His nose burned, his eyes smarted, his scalp itched. She's cauterizing the stone, he thought, oh yes, Lucienne called, swinging the bottle, wonderful, this stuff is wonderful! And she danced around the spitting, sizzling granite again and again. The Colonel vomited. At his back the graves went berserk and ran for cover, the gardeners turned blue in the face, pressed their palms to their temples, their mouths were gaping open, their teeth popping out—they sank to their knees, doubled over, their bodies twitching, but she, his wife, was suddenly wearing a gas mask, trumpeting a laugh through its snout, and laughing, she shook the last drops out of the bottle, still dancing, dancing around the grave that the corrosive liquid had fitted with a delicately trembling bubble so airy and transparent that it revealed all the colors of the rainbow, and burst them at the same time. He stood motionless, as if transfixed, and tried unsuccessfully to force the odorless dryness from his throat, and his face, just like the gardeners', now turned blue as well, violet, almost black, and his mouth opened to scream. Did he scream? Or was the firestorm that shook the willows louder than the explosion in his chest? He could still see the bombers retreating high in the air, and the dead trees, and then it became quiet, gray, and the first snow of winter sank down lightly, like ashes. "You, here?" he asked.

Lucienne was dabbing his forehead with a cloth. She sat on his bed, and didn't let go of his hand until morning.

The Colonel went down to the kitchen at noon. He wanted to thank his wife, he looked at the table, at the hearts and figures that Gerber had scratched there, and it took a long time, a strangely long time, for him to notice that the bottle of poison had disappeared. Lucienne was standing at the stove. Where was the bottle of poison? she repeated his question.

He nodded.

"You know," Lucienne said, "I've been thinking about it—let's leave the stone to the elements."

"And your poison assault?"

She smiled. "How you talk," she said.

There was a prolonged silence, but it meant nothing, it was the fear of the quiet that had invaded these rooms with their son's illness, that had closed their hearts and mouths.

She had poured out the poison, Lucienne said, took the teapot, and left the room.

VI

All Souls' Day, the long-awaited day of remembrance and family celebration, and the
anniversary of the burial, began exactly like a staff
exercise: the greeting of the daughters and step-
sons at the church, the joint attendance at a Mass
for the dead, the Captain at the altar. Then a walk
to the grave in silence. Prayer and remembrance.
Lights swimming in the morning mist, the gray
shadows of the cemetery visitors, a widow here,
a little group of people there, a crow cawing
somewhere. Then, right before they left, disaster,

paralysis, horror. Why hadn't she screamed? He stood there stooped over, grinning, shaking, old. Would she faint? No, no reaction, Lucienne maintained her composure. She bent down to the holy-water font, picked up a branch, made the sign of the cross. This was the signal to leave, one daughter after another stepped forward, dipped the branch in the water, handed it to the next one, and then the men followed, smiling, nodding to one another, they had learned this ritual the year before, it was to be repeated in the future, always on this day, and was to be handed down to their children, who would also get old in turn, as feeble as he, time, says the poet, is exact, and all-merciful.

"Shall we go?"

"Let's go."

Schacht, whom his wife called Motoff, assigned seats to the family in the automobiles they had with them. During which there was a brief skirmish involving the Casac, an attack of the gout, the old boy groaned, his hand on his side, it was clear he wanted to slip away, but Zizi, the very image of the future female head of the family, took him by the arm and steered him to the back seat of the Toyota, then jumped behind the wheel to head up the convoy. Setting the tempo, she chose the lake road, there was not a soul on the quay, the trees were bare, the gulls wheeling off in all directions, and farther out, where the fog was thicker, the light was cream-colored. The Colonel said nothing, he had surrendered. He was the last to board the *Laetitia*, she had already put to sea, and the day of grief and death filled the decks with life, which, as in the old days, smelled of coffee and cigar smoke and perfume. Eggs sizzled and water boiled in the galley, the Casac's first bursts of laughter could be heard shooting up to the dining-room ceiling, the daughters and sons-in-law joined in, there was brief applause. *Café complet*, the family called it, but really, the Colonel said to himself, that was incorrect, no one mentioned the fact that the host of grandchildren, the other daughters' brood, was excluded from the family gatherings due to Zizi's childlessness. She could not abide children. She said: I love children, God, how I love children, but at the same moment would press her palms to her temples, squint her eyes, a migraine, nothing to be done. Schacht, her husband, must carrry her out to the Toyota, after which, as Schacht reports, there follow hours of throwing up, yes, it's the weather, nothing major.

The Colonel rummages through the coats in the closet, searches the pockets quickly, someone, he hopes, will have left cigarettes there, the doctor has forbidden him to smoke, and his little phenol mouse is strict about that, she shows no mercy. He's happy to find some.

And how shall the thing be explained? Not by bringing Zizi into it, oh no. She will have told his sons-in-law that they shouldn't expect the old man to keep up with the kids' horsing around, her wish is their command, he sees his offspring seldom but that doesn't bother him, they're strangers to him, none of them carries his name, he is the last one, he, il Capitano, has outlived his son, and with him the family will die out, a drab, numbing fade-out, a downfall, but one that lacks glory. What remains shall be his name, a couple of dates, his rank and regiment, carved in stone.

He sits on the Gobelin stool in the entryway and sucks on a cigarette. He is warmed by the noisy life around him. His forehead is coated in oily sweat, but that's from the excitement, damn it, the Colonel says to himself, they got us this morning, a torpedo mid-ship, it's hopeless, the ship is going under.

"Hello, Papa!"

Gundi, a convert to anthroposophy, floats by in black knee socks and dark pleated skirt, her hair up in a braid, he smiles, has himself immediately under control and is able to hide the cigarette from his daughter, of course, in the cup of his hand.

"How are you, how are things?"

That was what he had always said to the rows of mountain infantry, his eyes checking their uniforms, collars, buttons, belts, and if they weren't close-shaven, he gave their fingernails a second going over, and even their teeth, then he immediately knew what was what. Let's see your gun barrel, come on, he says, it leaves something to be desired, the man stares at him, how could the old man have known that, he was never wrong, a bad tooth or a bit of dirt under the thumbnail points to rust or smoke buildup in the barrel, gives it away every time, leave canceled, next, how are you, how are things, but Gundi, without turning, has disappeared into the bathroom, she locks the door.

It could be, he thinks, that I'm getting a little eccentric with age. But wasn't that part of life? He had stuck his neck out for a cat, and had never been able to pet her, not even once. He longed, especially now, to feel her warmth on his hand, the murmur of her heart under her soft fur. He would have liked to speak to her, in human words, he sat on the stool blowing smoke out of his nose and looking at his fingernails, they were clean, of course, and suddenly he was sure that she would answer him with a grateful purr.

There was the sound of laughter coming from behind the doors.

It was laughable, but true—he wanted to protect her from death, and today, today of all days, with the entire family gathered at the grave, the unthinkable had happened, the catastrophe. At the foot of the gravestone, there for all to see, was the scrap of cellophane, ripped to shreds by her claws and teeth.

He hadn't trusted his wife, had always dealt with the possibility that she could launch her poison assault behind his back. He had wanted to avoid catastrophe: and it had come down on his head. Yesterday, on the evening before All Souls', he had buried a splendidly prepared apple, rolled in leaves and cellophane. He shook his head and grinned. Everyone had seen the scrap, they all knew—their grieving father went to the cemetery to feed a cat. A cat!

Outside the fog began to disperse. He blew the ashes which had fallen between his boots under the rug. They were opening champagne in the study, Veuve Cliquot, it's high time, the Casac called, that we take a few of the widows gathered on the buffet table and break their necks. His sons-in-laws greeted this pun with applause.

Schacht was the first to leave; he was taking the afternoon flight to the States. Gundi had reported that Papa was sitting in the entryway, but Schacht, already in hat and coat, returned to the group and said, smiling, that il Capitano had withdrawn, destination unknown. Schacht conveyed his regards and left.

The others left little by little. The mothers had to get back to their children, and the men were called back to their duties in the armories and barracks. Each couple promised to come again as soon as possible, by Christmas at the latest, and tooted good-bye as their cars left the park.

It was noon. Zizi reclined in Papa's armchair, the Casac stood in front of the bookshelves, he too was on his way.

"Are you looking for something in particular, my dear Captain?"

"There's not a philosophy title on the shelves, only military ones," the Casac remarked, "I can't understand why the old trooper is suddenly interested in Aristotle."

Zizi jumped up at this. "That's it, now I've had it!" she hissed. "Fine, please, just let him!

Let him hide. Let him act important. I couldn't care less! I really couldn't care less!" Zizi cried.

"*On a du style:* Remember your manners, my dear."

"Oh, right," Zizi said, "oh, right!" And quickly slipped into her flat shoes, grabbed the keys to the Toyota, her cigarettes and her handbag, and said good-bye to the Casac. "Shall I pick you up as always?"

"No," said Lucienne, "we'll stay here today." She offered her daughter her cheek, but her daughter gave her a kiss on the forehead. A minute later the Toyota shot out of the park. He too, the Casac said, had to go.

"Yes," Lucienne said, and smiled, "it makes me so happy to be able to sit here with you again as we used to, just the two of us."

The chaplain let out a soft sigh, sat back down obediently, and Lucienne refilled his glass.

The babies of society's elite live in Victoria's world. Their pillows are Victoria pillows, their bassinets Victoria bassinets, their dolls, their pacifiers, their bottles: Victoria. Victoria silk bonnets, modeled on a beekeeper's hat, protected their little bald heads from the sun, Victoria high chairs made eating fun, Victoria sleepers covered their absorbent Victoria diapers, Victoria baby boots encouraged them to walk, and it all had begun with the Victoria crawling pond, designed to rival the so-called playpen.

Before her son's death Lucienne, entrepreneur's daughter that she was, had helped Schacht found Victoria, providing advice and basic capital. The good Schacht loved the person closest to her heart; he too, she noticed, had spent his happiest hours in the summerhouse. She wanted to reward her son-in-law for that, and Lucienne rewarded him well. Behind the Colonel's back, she mortgaged the *Laetitia* up to its rafters, and it soon became apparent that Schacht was as successful and energetic at the office as he previously had been in the field. His strategic training had made an entrepreneur of him right off the bat. He made a gift of his first product, which he called the crawling pond, to every children's hospital in the country, and the promotional strategy worked—on all fronts at once. In a live TV broadcast from the cancer ward of the Children's Clinic in Zurich, little hairless creatures lay happily in a bright circle never before seen up to that time, the pond won a prize at the Geneva Inventors' Fair, the C. G. Jung Institute spotted mandalas in the water lilies, and Antje Mueller, the spiritualist, celebrated its victory over Catholic pedagogy. And after the well-known leftist, always-polemical journalist Meienberg bedded down his twins, born on Christmas Day, in a crawling pond—the picture made its way through the media—dentists and lawyers and instruction officers hastened to equip their houses with Victoria's baby-friendly, cheerful designs. His successful sales slogan was: focus on a limited market. By the baby's third year of life, the *New Zurich News* quoted Schacht, we will have reached our absolute limit, we are and shall remain outfitters for babies, designers for babies— let other companies take over at the walking and talking stages.

The *New Zurich News*, as Lucienne read with pleasure, judged Schacht's decision a wise one. It was true that the new bib got a rather disparaging review—the child was strapped into a sort of plastic metal jacket, the reporter wrote—but the same article endorsed the new high chair, the so-called Muesli Astronaut that had no straps or buckles at all, and it gave a guarded blessing to the already famous crawling pond that now was becoming a popular item. He himself, the reporter added, had had a very positive experience with the crawling pond; the depictions of the mushrooms and water lilies that decorated its circular bank had visibly advanced his son's tactile sense. "Nice," Lucienne said.

Zizi, of course, had not deemed it necessary to clip the article for her. She simply tossed her the paper after she had finished reading it, noting in passing that there was something in it about Schacht.

"Very nice," Lucienne repeated, smoothed the page which she carefully had torn out, and glued it in her album. The floor lamp next to her desk was on, and from somewhere close by or far away in the afternoon haze came the eternal sound of Meier-Labiche. The Casac had fallen asleep two hours ago. His Gottfried Benn-like head was drooping on the sofa arm, his mouth was open, and he was lightly snoring.

She had tried to talk to him, but the Casac, already drunk, didn't want to talk about the Colonel and the cat. He had said only that the country obviously was missing the collective suffering experienced in war. This meant that people were happy, but only as a people, the individual suffered alone, helplessly subject to his own private experience.

All in all, Lucienne thought, the day of remembrance and family celebration had been a success, harmonious and loving.

The Colonel, in his uniform, squatted on the wooden veranda that encircled the summerhouse a hand's width off the ground, like the floor of a carousel. Yellowing tufts of leaves poked through the slats and the wood was decaying—planks from a shipwreck. The ivy had lost its leaves and the vines that wrapped themselves around the carved columns looked like veins drained of blood. The Colonel knew that he had left his troops without permission. I should be tending to our guests, he thought. Water dripped from the trees, a gentle trickling sound, out on the lake a sea gull screamed now and then, and there was the sound of Meier-Labiche, of course—and its gassy smell. But the Colonel had grown accustomed to the factory that had been encroaching on the *Laetitia* for years. He smelled and heard it only when his eyes looked beyond the park and saw, over the brick wall to the north, the neon letters that flashed day and night. Now they swam in the evening light that floated over the works like an orange cloud.

Should he ask Meier-Labiche for help? They had both worked their way up from the bottom, they had both reached the top: Meier-Labiche, captain of industry, and he himself, il Capitano, who was about to lose his command and his ship. No, he thought, that wouldn't do, he couldn't ask his colleague to take over the feeding, he was the one she favored, she knew his voice, the smell of his leather coat, he alone was permitted to approach her. Gundi? Out of the question. Gundi had children, three or four or five, anthroposophists bred like rabbits, they had no time for cats. But his cat required her food! Damn it all, I can't just let the cat starve. He held a heavy key in his hand. He would stand up, put the key in the lock, and go into the summerhouse. Sooner or later, he said to himself, I have to go in and prepare tomorrow's ration, a double helping. If he were in battle—for a long time he looked up with longing into the bare treetops—he would be able to act: The battalion is ordered to retreat at the first opportunity.

My dear Gerber, thank you for everything, you were a good man.

Yes sir, Colonel sir.

A handshake, a pistol to his temple, salute, report of leave, fire. But Gerber was dead, years ago, and the iron object was not a military pistol but the key to the summerhouse. What was the solution? To fill the rucksack and then go to the cemetery and take off with the cat to the mountains? He could reach his former area of operations, he reckoned, in two days of strenuous marching. He knew every stone there, every furrow, every hut. He could spend the winter there on some Alpine farm or other, far from everyone. There was only one problem: Supplies. You understand? We have no one to bring us supplies.

The neon letters became brighter, night was coming on. The cat, he felt, understood him. Death by starvation is a bad death. The Colonel stood up. I must find a way to keep you from going to the grave every day, bony and trembling as you were when I found you, whimpering and crying like the soul of a dead child. Do you understand? And again she understood him. We'll make it quick, he said, quick and painless. Then the key fell from his hand and the ground rose up to meet him, he heard a crash, a splintering, and then it was dark.

The stove hadn't been lit for days. The crackling, said the women in black, reminded the dying of purgatory. They sat at the dining-room table saying the rosary, and put their dentures, which looked like shiny red toads, on the oilcloth so that their clacking wouldn't disturb his voyage into the next world. From time to time one of the women stood, sighing, to dip a cloth in a bowl, wring it out, and wipe his father's face.

They had placed his bed in the drawing room. When the sun began to come up, the boy was told to kneel down, his father put his hand on his head and began to talk. There was a gingerbread cookie in the cabinet. It wasn't one of the best kind, wasn't filled with honey and crusted with sprinkles, but, the father said, it was gingerbread. He would not tolerate the auctioneer eating the gingerbread as well. Then hands reached out for him, he must pray now, they said, their teeth were back in their mouths, one of them stroked his cheek, and one of them he didn't know, quietly commented that the cold had set in. Father's soul had gone out the window, with the cold. Then the carpenter came. He was to measure his father for his last garment, he said, and the boy had to laugh. That evening he was taken to the parsonage, farmers sat along the walls, he had to say the Lord's Prayer and the priest scratched the sign of the cross on his forehead, mouth, and chin with a ragged thumbnail. Fine, a low voice said, he liked him, he'd take him. At that the farmers stood up and went out. The boy remained with the priest until the funeral, then he was taken back to the cold room, he was to wait there, Stauffer would come for him. He sat on the bench next to the heater for a long time, then he climbed up to the cupboard, opened the glass door, felt around in the dark for the gingerbread cookie, and quickly ate it. In the middle of the night there was a thumping sound. It was Stauffer, his uncle, who threw himself down on the deathbed and poured seven Christmases' worth down his throat at one gulp, as he put it. The dead man, he said, had been a miserly bastard, who, over the years, had doled out the schnapps a little at a time on special occasions, then he laughed and took a swig from the bottle. Stauffer dressed him in one of his father's smocks and pulled him out into the frosty cold. The path was hard and glistened. Whenever he stepped on the smock's hem and fell, Stauffer would laugh, Judgment Day, he called, Cheers, Savior and Sons, it's all one big hoax, Stauffer was already looking forward to it.

At Stauffer's farm he was given a little room under the roof. Owls often came in through the attic window, fluttering against the wind, and the boy thought of the souls that flew through the window without cutting themselves on the glass. A tomcat slept lying across his neck at night, it kept him warm and he managed to hide the cat from Stauffer. For Stauffer fed all the cats calves' milk, and when they were two years old, he would slaughter and marinate them. They tasted good, he said, better than rabbit. First he ate the liver, then the roasted flesh.

The dogs often started to bark long before the morning wake-up call was given. Then the boy would know that Stauffer was lying outside, stretched out on the ground with his shirt sticking to his body, his head bloody. That was it with guzzling schnapps, Stauffer would groan, then he would crawl into the fountain trough head first, dragging his legs along like a crocodile its tail. The boy milked and fed the cows early each morning, and if Stauffer had come to again by then he would go to the vat and lift the lid; the milk was rich, foaming with creamy flecks. It smelled of the warm shed, with its cow dung.

Stauffer drank more and more; he would wrap his meals in a handkerchief, his appetite, he said, improved in the stalls. But one day the boy stumbled over three sacks filled with stale bread and half-eaten sausages. Then he knew that Stauffer's end was nigh, the only thing going down his throat was liquid.

When someone in the village died, Stauffer was hired as grave digger. The two of them—the primary school's best pupil and the sweaty schnapps drinker no one spoke to anymore—would dig the grave. They packed the bones and skulls that they dug up with the clumps of earth into Stauffer's rucksack—later they ground them into meal, packaged it in bags, and sold it to the parsonage. When Stauffer died, the boy dug his grave. He put the quarter-pound of coffee beans that he had received as payment into Stauffer's coffin with him. Stauffer had been killed by a fir tree that he had felled himself.

He was sent to the city, to Lucerne. He was thirteen then, in secondary school and eligible for public support, but too old for the orphanage. So he was given a bed and his meals in the home for the deaf and dumb. He had to rise each morning at three. The director's wife knew only one method of waking anyone: she grabbed the sleeping boy by the shoulders with both hands and shook him awake. She never spoke a word. When he opened his eyes she shuffled out of the room in her felt slippers.

In the summer he rode the director's bicycle outside the city, where he would pedal from farm to farm to offer the deaf-mutes as labor to the farmers. They would be squatting on their milk stools when he entered the dark stables, and soon he got better commissions than had the director. He understood cattle, the farmers said. Then he would return to the home and sit at the table watching the deaf-mutes eat while the director's wife made coffee with milk. They never spoke, but it was noisy at meals nevertheless—they slurped and smacked their lips, and farted and burped. They couldn't help it. Their ears, the director's wife said one morning, were only holes. Her name was Gertrude.

After breakfast he led them to the fields. The deaf-mutes were paid a daily wage for harvesting crops and hay. That, he later said, is how he learned to give orders—with his eyes. Words, good God, no one would hear them in the heat of battle!

He was shunned by his schoolmates. He was a stranger to them, someone from the mountains who scratched out his spelling mistakes with his thumbnail and fell asleep during class breaks. He was always tired. During the summer he pedaled out to the farmers early each morning, and in the winter he had to light the stoves each day to earn his keep. He performed this duty freezing, shaking with the cold. First he cleaned the cinders from all of the boilers and lit the kindling, then he shoveled in the coal he had carried up from the cellar, one wheelbarrow at a time. When the last stove was lit it was already time to stoke the first one again, and his body, which had been freezing only shortly before, was now burning, sweating, breaking out in welts and festering pustules and scabs that his classmates laughed at. But it was strange—as much as he hated that hell, that freezing, burning cellar, he looked forward to each load that roared and burned like wildfire in the boiler, for in springtime, on the day his boiler work was ended for the season, he would go into the kitchen and a potato pie topped with cheese would be steaming on the table, and there would be slices of juicy pear, a bottle of white wine, and Gertrude standing at the long stove saying: "Eat, you've earned it."

One day a young vicar addressed him. He had a double cross to bear, the vicar said to him. Did he understand what he meant by that, he asked.

The boy said yes, that the vicar meant, first, the cross of Christ at Golgotha, and second, the cross on the national flag.

"Excellent," the vicar said. "Someone like you belongs in school. I'll see to it. You may go."

When he left the home, Gertrude was standing at the kitchen window and the director had to shoo the deaf-mutes, who were waving rags and dishcloths, back into the building. He graduated in early summer, 1939. The next day he entered officers training school, there was already talk of war, and he decided that he would be one of the first to fall.

VII

It was as if eternal winter had set in, trees and cars and people were frozen solid, like ice, in the stillness of death. No movement, no sound, and yet one could still see in the land, the objects, and the people what they once had been. People waited on platforms for trains to arrive, frozen in mid-step; three train workers stood on the loading ramp with rolled-up signal flags under their arms, and the upper half of an engineer's body was leaning out the side window of his switching car. Conductor line poles were bent, some had been torn from their foundation. And one train was lying on the embankment. In the city, buildings were lying on their sides. And a row of trees had keeled over along the lake shore, boats in the bight were covered, Bahnhof Strasse was empty of people, there was an ambulance sitting at Postplatz with its tailgate open and a coffin inside, and the puffs of smoke coming out of the chimneys hung motionless in the air. Wherever one looked there was dead matter, felled with one stroke, switched off. Despite this, some things had maintained themselves, as if saving themselves for the dawn of a new era—a piece of landscape here, a row of villas there, below them the *Laetitia*, and high above the city, higher than the church towers still standing, the glowing letters of MEIER-LABICHE. The factory too, with its glass roofs, its halls, and its latticework fences and concrete surfaces, all of these, except for a bit of damage, were intact, including the entire train station, right down to the details, down to the boxes of geraniums hanging from the platform roofs, tiny, to be sure, but visible in the dental mirror that Zizi had given her brother as a present.

The lake was a piece of cathedral glass. Schacht had cut it, joined it, and tinted it a dark green, then scattered bits of silver tinsel on it so that, depending on the light, the waves glinted and seemed to move. A change in the wind and the hard surface was broken through, the layer of dust became ice, it sparkled and flashed, but the Colonel quickly closed the door again, the lake disappeared, it became dark, and in this nocturnal world, which took up almost the entire floor of the summerhouse, the pots of clay and paint rose up like cooling towers. Their contents were hard as rocks, the brushes stiff, and in one corner, piled up to the domed ceiling, were boxes full of tracks, locomotives, cars, switches, and signal posts that Schacht had given his brother-in-law as the boy was dying. Work had stopped shortly after the last of it was delivered, and the half-completed project began to gather dust.

The Colonel held his breath. He heard footsteps in the gravel, the door opened, once again there was light in the summerhouse, and for a long time he and Lucienne stood facing one another.

Nothing happened. She smiled. Then she sat down on his cot, which still stood next to the door. The Colonel stepped across the city and the lake, smashing a house, a switch, and opened a window, then strained against the shutters—they were nailed shut with boards from the outside—there was a cracking, a splintering, a splitting sound, and then, suddenly, in the middle of the Alps that were painted on the walls, a spring day emerged, the twittering of birds, and a blinding light streamed in through the window.

The west shore, a hilly outline at the foot of the Alps, remained a ruin in the making. A plotted tangle of wooden pieces formed the skeleton of the hills, it was true, but the tops were covered only in wire mesh, it was a landscape without meadows, and to the south, at the end of the fjord-like bay where his former area of operations began, the few rock formations (cork) and a blurred line of mountain and sky (drawn on the wall with charcoal pencil) gave only a vague idea of the mass that was the Gotthard Tunnel. The Colonel stopped where he was, he was acquainted with every single rock here. Then he slid down the wall to the floor, remained seated there with his boots in the lake, and looked at his wife, who rose behind the city like a mountain, black, mute, old. Love at last sight, thought the Colonel, and Lucienne grinned at him as if she had read his mind.

The city lay in the center of the summerhouse, directly beneath the dome, and offered a view of the creation of such a project in all its phases. A shell here, an unoccupied building there, and right next to it the finished model of the shore paths (cardboard strips); the lanterns along the quay were made of wire nails, arced at the top, using a bit of clay as a cap. The tree trunks were carpenter's nails wrapped in bark, and their crowns, some painted, some only roughly formed, were cotton balls soaked in a lotion that the captain of the medical corps, who dropped by every day, had left with his patient. All of these tiny details had been painstakingly created under a magnifying glass; the only things they had ordered by mail were the pedestrians and the train workers, with flesh-colored ovals for faces, and the trains, the tracks, and the so-called accessories (signals, switches, crossing gates).

The next day they returned again, and sat in the summerhouse until dusk dimmed the plastic valleys with their blue shadows, and the last light faded on the white south wall. The Colonel then offered his wife his arm. They set off for the *Laetitia*, the sultry sound of a French horn wafted in from the lake, then frenzied shouting—the excursion steamer wailed by full of yodelers, male and female, and grinning, the Colonel pointed back over his shoulder into the park. A bush of white roses sparkled like snow in the darkness.

Their visits to the summerhouse replaced their visits to the grave. They drank their tea at three every afternoon, just as before, and then the Colonel gave their marching orders. Their skin hung on them like clothes that came to look more and more alike as the months went by. Time ran backward, only the past was still alive. They could laugh about that, and talk for hours, and if their conversation trickled over into the early evening they dreamed their old stories again, back to the time of their youth and childhood, which for him was a mountainous region full of overhangs and inclines, and for her was a land of huge trees, hurried along by male secretaries wearing glasses and carrying briefcases. Then Lucienne would look out into the park through the Alpine window and become almost confused, for its state of neglect had returned the grass, the bushes, and the trees to its splendor and glory as seen through the eyes of her childhood. Time was erased in the wild growth, and the *Laetitia* lay like a seaworthy ship at anchor in the bay of some unexplored archipelago.

At some point, the first train departed. It slipped into the tunnel, all its car windows lit up, it emerged from the mountain farther up, and the transformers, housed within the Meier-Labiche plant, emitted a soft, realistic, humming sound. The Colonel lay on his stomach on the lake, his hands reaching through the gates of the factory (they closed around his arms like cuffs) into the inside of the factory, and soon his fingers got the hang of the switches and buttons and levers, normal traffic, almost without incident. He had an overview of the tilted control board through the glass roof of the assembly hall, and toward evening, when the colored lamps shone inside and his dark hands covered the board like a giant octopus setting up more and more transportation lines, he saw from his wife's posture that she was in the hospital, lost in thought beside the incubator with its tiny bundle lying inside, which was hooked up to plastic tubes. My son, he had said then, can beat death.

"Shall we go?"

"Let's go."

The bitter period of grief was over. They became more and more contented here, beneath this dome of heaven, which during the course of the afternoon created a sundial over land, lake, and boxes. Switches clicked, bells rang at crossing-gates, people waited on the platforms, the excursion ship docked at the quay, Lucienne sat on the cot wrapped in scarves, and the Colonel, with his officer's coat covering him, lay on the lake. He thought ever more often of that winter night, the wind howling, when the three of them, he, his son, and Schacht, laid the north-south track and macadamized it with shavings from their lead pencils. That was the first time he had entered the summerhouse, and—whether it was that the strategist was fascinated by the project's creation, or that his terminally ill son had disobeyed his father's orders finally to come to bed—the Colonel too had knelt down in the landscape in the end and helped the two builders finish the last stretch that night. Because the track led up into the Alps, it had been his idea to add troops in battle formation, from the midlands to the mountains, and two or three months after his first visit they decided to execute this plan. Their work was interrupted as they were putting in the horse-drawn wagons (with tweezers). Schacht carried his son over to the house. A car pulled up shortly thereafter, someone hurried across the gravel, apparently the captain of the medical corps, there was the sound of excited voices and then it was quiet. The Colonel remained alone in the summerhouse, sitting on the east bank of the lake and bawling like a child. At his feet was an unfinished world, smelling of paint and clay, with wire and soldering irons and screwdrivers lying about. All the trains were still. The Colonel, in order to have something to do, crawled around on all fours pulling cords out of their sockets.

"Shall we go?"

"Let's go," he said, took his cane, and leaning

on his wife's arm, stooped over, shuffled back to the house at her side, pushing one foot in front of the other. This single path that he still trod grew longer with each day. By the time they finally reached the steps, it was dark.

One afternoon they heard Zizi's horn, it had become impossible for cars to get through, there were broken branches lying about, twigs everywhere, and the gravel drive had become a meadow overgrown with weeds.

As Lucienne later determined, Zizi had gone into the boat shed and cranked the old rowboat out of the water. Long and heavy beards of algae hung from the keel. They had dried over the course of the summer and become gray braids, crawling with mosquitoes that increased in number, became myriad, and swarmed about each other in swirling masses. Lucienne liked their shrill singsong, interrupted now and then by a swallow sailing through or a fish rushing to the surface to balance on its tail for a second, snap its jaws, and splash back down into the muddy, metallic water, the churning water, full of life. If she tossed away a piece of bread it immediately was covered with beetles, the reeds were full of the sounds of breeding, and Lucienne, laughing and singing, danced through the hip-high grass of the flat bank.

Il Capitano sat in a wheelchair behind the terrace balustrade. His head was sunk to his chest, but nevertheless he appeared able to hear her—he waved with the butterfly net.

There was a humming in the air everywhere, a buzzing and stirring, ducks rose up suddenly with a loud beating sound, their fat wings created a sucking and snapping, a shoving and striking, Come on, and above her, powdered in moonlight, his strong shoulders, damp forehead, his nose making snorting sounds, Wait, she manages to stammer, braces the lower part of her body, raises herself from the sticky plastic seat—yes, that's right, it was in the old Chevy, up on the Furka Pass, she lay in his arms, the war was raging in the mountains outside, the sound of saluting guns, of machine guns, cries, screams, his regiment was advancing, figures—bent over—raced by the car windows, antennae whipping around on their backs, she dug her fingers into his flesh, laughing, then screaming: Come.

Lucienne watched the birds change course. It would be five soon, high time for some tea.

She pushed her husband into the study, tied a napkin around him, filled a baby bottle with

whiskey, and let him sip at it. He did not consider
the bottle a humiliation: his hands trembled as if
the bones had been removed from his speckled
skin. But the Colonel prided himself on being
able to drink without her help—after all, he had
said in one of the last sentences they could understand, he had been a supply officer. Sup-ply.
Sup-, and with his last strength, his body shaking: -ply. At that point Lucienne understood that
her husband's reason was stealing away now as
well, he even appeared to have forgotten his rank
and regiment, the most important thing in the
world to him. The sips that he took spilled back
out of his mouth again, but it didn't matter, not
really—the beard gave him the dignified appearance of an elderly captain.

It was pleasantly cool inside, despite the fact
that it was high summer. Ivy had begun to grow
over the windows, and it almost seemed to her
as if this ribbon of half-light that was wrapping
itself around the *Laetitia* gave the air a gentle blue
tinge.

Lucienne leafed through an album. Sometimes she laughed softly, and if he raised his head
a bit she would roll his wheelchair next to the
arm of the sofa, and lay the open book on his
lap. Here we are, getting married. This is Zizi
being baptized. This is the young captain with

his first company. In this one Fonti, later commander of the division, is shaking hands with him, victorious after the field maneuvers at Rheinwaldhorn, its peak in the clouds. Here is the battalion commander in his helmet, Gerber at the edge of the picture, and here, my God, that's Fonti's wife, blond as Marilyn Monroe, her sunglasses on top of her head and a Gitane between her fingers, a staff field trip through Normandy, the picnic at the Atlantic Line, to the left the bunker, the Casac drunk in the sand, and here, she had to laugh again, our youngest daughter's baptism, Zizi, the eldest, with tears in her eyes, she had lost her purse somewhere, no, that was later, and here—son, he tried to say.

She stroked his cheek. Good man. At dusk she filled the baby bottle again, with a burning black rum this time. She had inherited the bottles from her father; they came from below the equator—they had, as sailors said, crossed the Line. That was the Sundowner. Outside the humming died down, the chirping stopped, and soon the quiet aboard the *Laetitia* was so deep that it seemed to transform itself into the droning of motorboats, a tremulous racket, full speed ahead, toward the star high up in the southern sky, a point in the unending blue among the dark night foliage.

After the Colonel's death, Lucienne moved to the Tessin; she sold the *Laetitia*. She lived alone and went walking along the lake every evening, looking for a bride for her son who had been dead for ten years now, and who remained a small child in her dreams. Would that blonde over there make a good match for him? Or that one, sitting on the railing? A little too plump from behind, but men like that, they all like that.

"Remember your manners," Lucienne ordered herself, looked away and walked on.